Seeing her for the first time, looking like a walking hot sex dream, had him almost undone.

Billionaire Tycoon Grant Hamilton stared down at the woman sleeping atop of his white, Egyptian cotton bed linens.

Fiery red hair tousled around a sensual face, long lashes casting shadows over rosy cheeks. Her hands rested between her creamy curvy legs, partially covering her half naked, luscious body. Soon to be his wife.

Maybe
Probably
Hopefully…

Her body…her body was making him sweat. Those perfectly made for sin curves. His shaft hardened.

She was just the way he liked his women, heaving bosom and a bottom a man could grab a hold of. One look at her and a man knew she would be a firecracker when her passions were unleashed. Yesterday had been more than enough proof of that.

BOOKS BY MONTANA NIGHT

BILLIONAIRE BROTHERS: HAMILTON

The Russian Mail-Order Bride
The Stand-In Bride
The Tycoon's Replacement Bride Part 1
The Tycoon's Replacement Bride Part 2
The Tycoon's Replacement Bride Part 3

Sign up to the author's newsletter for special offers and book updates:

mnightmailingoptin.labelleauboisdormant.co.uk

THE TYCOON'S

Replacement Bride

[COMPLETE TRILOGY]

MONTANA NIGHT

For queries, comments or feedback please contact La Belle Au Bois
Dormant Publishing.

www.labelleauboisdormant.co.uk
info@labelleauboisdormant.co.uk

Printed in the United Kingdom

ISBN-13: 978-1-909916-41-8

ACKNOWLEDGMENTS

To my husband, because *he is the wind beneath my wings*. To my mother because without her I would never have been. To my friends because their encouragement was invaluable. To my readers for loving my books. To you all I say thank you.

Montana Night

MONTANA NIGHT

PART 1

CHAPTER 1

Amanda Cardwell sunk down into her seat, feeling like the most improbable mail-order bride of all time. She rode the tram tracks into Orlando International Airport, and her auburn locks glinted in the sunshine streaming through the tram car window. She could feel the cool air conditioning mixed with the warm tropical breeze caressing her curvy legs.

She was clinging to her most important items, Louis Vuitton handbag in one hand, iPhone in the other. Her luggage from the flight was carry-on only.

Amanda let out her breath slowly. *I still can't believe Emma talked me into this.* Although she had agreed to help her best friend Emma Baker by taking her place as a mail-order bride, Amanda couldn't stop thinking that this was a new all-time low.

She had been on a roll lately, racking up a depressing string of romantic misfires. "*That's me - Amanda Cardwell, Senior Lab Chemist and Senior Loser in Love, formally known to date various addicts, cheats, and secretly married men,"* she thought to herself as the tram settled at the terminal. Her last spectacular disaster was seven months ago. His name was Scott Schermer. A Wall Street broker who had a thing for full-figured redheads, and hiding his wedding ring.

That had been the last straw. She finally had enough of liaisons. She couldn't stand being in yet another relationship where she wasn't valued or appreciated.

To get her mind off the Scott fiasco, Amanda used up her vacation days during the summer months partying it up with Emma. They had reverted to their former party days in a way that they hadn't done since college. It was a crazy summer. They went on a road trip travelling around watching live music whilst bunking in Emma's truck. They even ended up along the coast where they rented a boat for a short trip down river. Summer whizzed away in a haze of drunken nights filled with endless jugs of sangria and even a few intimate moments with hunky strangers. Then Emma had gone ahead and done the unthinkable: she had fallen in love.

Gone off the deep end. Amanda bit her lower lip. She *was* happy for her friend. However it brought home the fact that although she was fast approaching 30, she had no serious relationship and her biological clock was ticking away.

A new chat message blinked in on her phone.

"DID YOU MAKE IT THERE OK? CALL ME!"

Amanda crossed her leg, tossed her amber hair over her shoulder, and hit speed dial. A man reading the newspaper glanced her way momentarily. His eyes lingered on her pin-up legs before sticking his face back behind the sports section.

"Hello, Amanda? Is that you?" Emma sounded far away.

"Yes, it's me." Amanda started rubbing her forehead. "I am freaking out. This is a bad idea. What if I get kidnapped at this Billionaire's house? What's he going to do when he sees that I am not you?"

Of all the things that had come out of Amanda's mouth, the last statement was without a doubt the one she dreaded the most. Emma was supermodel slim with looks to match. Although a madcap adventure to a billionaire's mansion was right up Amanda's alley *(she was on a roll after all)* being compared to a Cameron Diaz look-a-like and found lacking wasn't.

"Just do it the way we rehearsed. It's bulletproof," Emma said with an impatient sigh.

Amanda took a deep breath and tried to remember why the hell she was putting herself through all this.

Truth be told Emma was like a sister to her. It all started over 12 years ago. They met each other on her very first day at Babson College in Massachusetts. They hit it off right away. Whether it was studying in the science lab, drinking at Beat the Clock, or hot steamy dorm room nights with cute reporters from the Communications Block, they had become inseparable friends. Today that friendship was being tested to its limits. Amanda took another deep breath.

"Let me get this straight, just one more time for the record. You met a guy on-line on a dating site, and he turns out to be a CEO/Billionaire/Lonely spinster. And so you get him on a web cam, flash your legs and probably show him your pussy galore -"

"Amanda! I did no such thing. Believe you me, I wanted to.

We just didn't get that far." Emma laughed out loud.

The man reading the newspaper glanced in Amanda's direction *again*. His eyes lingered suggestively on her ample bosom before sticking his face back behind the sports section. *Note to self, don't talk about pussy out loud on a packed tram.*

"Great." Amanda rolled her eyes. "So then he sends you 50 thousand bucks and asks you to marry him…."

"Right."

"And then you went ahead and spent all the money last summer when we tore up New York and the Hampton's."

"It's not about the money Amanda. Tony is the man of my dreams. We have a special connection. There's no way I can go through with the mail-order wedding now!"

"Emma for God's sake, you are completely hopeless. You shouldn't have agreed to it to begin with. It's not like you need to beg men to date you."

"If you weren't my best friend I would never have agreed to this. Can't believe I've got to go and break it to this rich guy that you are not going to marry him. What were you thinking, spending his $50,000 dowry? What if he kidnaps me or has me put in jail or something?"

"He's not going to kidnap you, he's a billionaire."

Amanda snorted derisively. Clearly Emma had an unrealistic expectation of men in power positions. Amanda's experience had shown her they could be just as bad as your average Joe. Cue a flashback to Wall Street philandering scum Scott.

"He's not going to put you in jail. Just make sure you get to him tonight. Don't forget to call me and let me know what the estate is like! If he flips out because you're the wrong woman, just jump in a cab and stay down at the Hampton Inn. You'll get a free vacation. The $1500 I gave you should cover the room, the travel and the flight back to Philly."

"I can't believe you even had that much of it left." *We should have given it back and pleaded for a down payment scheme.* It was too late now.

Emma paused, and then said, "Amanda, who knows you might hit it off. He's into all that Biotechnology stuff. You guys can talk about curing cancer and DNA splicing."

"I don't remember you being such a hopeless romantic. He will take one look at me, his replacement, big bosom, curvy bottom, mail-order bride and send me packing. This is going to be so humiliating. Good thing I am a big girl, literally. I can suck it up. But you are going to owe me big."

Emma let out a sigh of relief. "Thanks for doing this babe, you are a lifesaver. Don't forget to look out for the limo sign that says my name!"

A bell sounded and the announcer indicated for passengers to disembark.

"I've got to go. I'll call you when I get there." Amanda made sure she didn't trip on her heels as she made her way onto the moving airport escalator. *Just another unplanned adventure.*

CHAPTER 2

Just like in the TV shows, there was a large man in black sunglasses and white gloves holding up a sign with her best friend's name written on it. The chauffeur helped her put the luggage in the trunk, and then looked around for the rest of her bags. "Travelling light today," she said sheepishly.

The drive out to the estate was quiet and very sunny. She counted palm trees and watched as the various resort signs whizzed by. The air conditioner was working diligently all the while. The black leather of the car seat soothed her sore back. *I've never been good at relaxing on planes.*

Amanda's mind wandered as the car drove past the restaurants and billboard signs. She thought of Scott, the adulterer. She had a hard time accepting that he misled her about his married life for almost six months. That and the fact that he had 2 children! Amanda still felt ashamed that she hadn't caught on earlier. She wasn't a home wrecker. She had broken it off with Scott the night that he told her. She still couldn't believe the douchebag waited until after they'd had steamy, hot sex before revealing his secret. *What do you expect from a man?*

Her mind travelled back with idle precision. He was a scumbag, but she had to admit that she had fallen in love with him. She had seen what she wanted to see instead of his true colors. He had been completely lacking in gentlemanly behavior. Hindsight really was a bitch.

She remembered how he wouldn't bother holding the door open for her or help her carry her bags. He believed in equality. This of course also meant he used to try to make her pay the check when they went out for dinner. The guy had been loaded for heaven's sake! What a cheapskate! Why had she put up with it?

The sex, that's why. It could not be denied. They had some great, long, pleasure filled nights. She would never admit to this out loud (no self-respecting feminist would), but she had a thing for powerful, sexually, dominating men. She was drawn to them like a moth to a flame. Scott had been 100% alpha in bed. *All that man-whoring experience must have come in handy.*

He would rest his large hand on her thigh as he drove her miles out of town in his Lexus. His hand would inevitably rise up her curved thigh, find its way to her panties, and then to the closely cropped fiery red patch between her legs. She would lay back in the seat as Scott would get to work, pushing his thick fingers coated with pussy juices rhythmically as far as he could between her legs, rubbing her clit whilst–.

The fast moving limo hit a small pothole, and Amanda was startled out of her daydream. The shiny, glass screen embedded in the seat rest sprang to life. The familiar *Skype* logo paused in center screen for a moment, followed by a series of chirps. She stared at the screen for a moment, and then intuitively pressed a single glossy black button that was inset into its frame.

The device chirped a quick response and blinked twice. A handsome, rugged looking man was staring at her with an odd intensity.

"Hello?" she said, struggling for a moment to sit up straight in the limo's black leather bucket seats.

"Good day Ms. Watson. This is Marcus Davidson calling on behalf of the estate of Grant Hamilton. I wanted to welcome you to the Sunshine Coast. I trust your flight was brief and uneventful?"

"The journey was fine." Amanda didn't know what to say. "It was really, really, err-uneventful. Please call me eh – Emma."

Marcus smiled briefly. "You are about 30 minutes from the estate grounds. Please enjoy the complimentary refreshments in the bar. There's sparkling water, soft drinks, and champagne."

"Oh, thank you Mr. Davidson - that's very kind."

"Please call me Marcus. I wanted to take the opportunity to inform you that Mr. Hamilton will not be present at the estate tonight."

How odd.

"I'm sorry to hear that. Did something come up?"

"He's been called to Switzerland on important company business. But rest assured, he has asked me to make sure you are feeling welcome here at the estate, and shown a good time until he returns."

"Oh, I'm sure you will. Thank you Mr. Davidson – I mean Marcus."

This isn't what I was expecting, Amanda thought, sinking down in her seat. *Not only do I have to face the firing squad, but I will have wait overnight at some rich guy's house before my execution.*

"Oh, Emma."

"Yes?"

"You might want to straighten your attire." With those cryptic words the screen went dark.

Amanda looked down on herself. Her dress had ridden up. From his vantage point, Marcus Davidson would have been looking straight at her black panties. She felt herself turn red from head to toe. *Darn, what must he be thinking of me!*

***

AFTER ANOTHER THIRTY-MINUTE limousine ride the car pulled up to a magnificent estate. Amanda began to feel acutely anxious. Row upon row of lined trees, and perfectly trimmed hedges offered privacy to this magnificent Florida manor. The house had a facade of sand stone, and the back end of the house came to an impressive and intimidating point, overlooking the ocean and seaside valley.

Amanda, please calm yourself down, she thought as the car pulled up in front of the house. *When they realize you are not Emma — the fabled Billionaire Grant Hamilton will cancel the whole affair.*

She picked a small vodka bottle from the bar fridge and drank it down like she was in the Navy. *Time for a little liquid courage,* she thought. Then she stepped out of the car to face her host.

CHAPTER 3

The man from the Skype call was standing at the front steps of the massive house to welcome her. *OMG.* He might have looked good on the screen, but up close and personal he was drop dead gorgeous.

"Emma. Welcome to the Hamilton Estate. I am Marcus Davidson, we spoke earlier. I am the estate's caretaker. I am sure you are very tired from traveling, and I suspect you might want to relax before dinner."

At the sound of his deep rumbling voice Amanda trailed her eyes up to his and her heart stopped. He stood on the front steps of the mansion, muscled arms crossed. He looked like a beautiful warrior promising wicked delights and fulfilling sweaty nights. Was that a glint of appreciation in his eyes? *My heart, be still.*

"Let me show you where you will be staying."

He waved his arm, and two helpers sprung forward to take her bags. One of the helpers, a muscular African American with short shaved hair, let his eyes linger around her curvy waist for a moment before tipping his head and grabbing her carry-on.

They walked briskly through the gardens down a cobblestone path. He walked like a panther, all grace and sexual possession.

"So, do you know when Mr. Hamilton is coming back? I'm his…ehhm — mail-order bride. I was only planning to be here for a day. I wasn't expecting the house to be empty."

Marcus turned around and gave her an appraising look. Amanda was mesmerized. His eyes were the color of dark chocolate with flecks of hazelnut.

"I can see that you are disappointed. I actually know very little about the situation, other than I was told to take you around and show you all the grounds and areas that Mr. Hamilton thought you might like."

His gaze travelled slowly up her pin up legs, lingered on her curvy waist and ample tits before settling on her lush lips. Amanda felt like covering herself. She wasn't supermodel thin, but she had never been more aware of that then at this precise moment. Stand up straight. *No man ever married an insecure woman.* Her Grandmother's advice echoed in her mind. Not that she was trying to marry Marcus.

"You, know, it's interesting…I wasn't shown your picture. The other staff and I were hoping that you would see the sign at the airport; otherwise, we probably never would have found you."

So that's why he hasn't thrown me out into the street. Her fear prickled up. *Time to change the subject.*

"The place is absolutely beautiful," she said, admiring the gardens, meanwhile with one eye checking out Marcus's body. He had strong, chiseled muscles beneath that shirt. "You must love being here."

"It's my home. Who could ask for more?"

"Shall I assume that you will be staying until Mr. Hamilton returns tomorrow?" He seemed to be holding his breath.

Amanda's mind was racing. The need to leave was tugging at her, but she had promised Emma. One overnight stay wouldn't hurt. Besides, she felt a strange pull to get to know Marcus a little bit better. There was something about him. She couldn't put her finger on it though.

"We've prepared the guesthouse for you. Please follow me." He started walking away.

Before she could think better of it, Amanda ran after him, letting curiosity get the better of her.

When they reached the guesthouse, Marcus helped bring her bags to her room, and invited her to an early supper. The guesthouse was done up like a farmhouse, with painted white cabinets and slab stone floor in the kitchen, lots of wood paneling and rustic fixtures. *This is a villa in its own right.*

"There are fresh towels upstairs and down. There's a fully stocked bar and fridge, as well as HDTV." Marcus spoke as he showed her the kitchen area. "And, here is the home security panel." Marcus drew her attention to a small digital screen beside the phone in the kitchen. "You can press this button to contact the kitchen in the main building. And this one shows you the cameras around the estate."

She nodded, somewhat nervously. The idea of cameras reminded her she was an intruder here, or at least someone who was here under false pretenses.

"This button is the important one. You can call me directly." He pointed at the blue button.

"Thank you, Marcus." she smiled at him. I think I will take a shower now and rest before our tour continues."

"Of course. Call the house if you need anything." Marcus bowed slightly.

Finally alone to contemplate her ruse, Amanda undid the clasp of her necklace and stepped out of her sandals.

As she took her dress off, she caught a look of her reflection in the mirror. Her full, curvy figure was highlighted by her black lace briefs. Her arms and neck were slightly freckled a curse of her red head complexion. As she surveyed herself, she grimaced and decided this was not the day to whip out the magnifying glass.

Wary she tiptoed into the bathroom, fished out her iPhone and a pack of Marlboro Menthol, and lit one while sitting on the toilet. She dialed Emma, hoping to catch her before she went to work.

"Hello?" Emma sounded half asleep.

"Emma, you are never going to believe this. This guy, Hamilton, your big new husband-to-be— is not even here. I am sitting in the guesthouse, getting shown around by some hot mystery man."

"That doesn't sound too bad, in my opinion."

"I have to stay here overnight! That was not the plan. What if they figure out I am not you!"

"This strange house guy, what did he say his name was?"

"It's Marcus." She exhaled a plume of smoke toward the bathroom window. *Gotta stop smoking every time I get flustered.*

"What's that noise? Are you smoking?" Amanda sighed heavily and put out her cigarette. Damn Emma and her superhuman hearing.

"Nope, just taking a deep breath. Don't be so suspicious." *Shouldn't have agreed to that no-smoking pact.*

"So is Marcus single? Remotely interested? And did you say he

13

is the butler?"

"Don't be daft Emma, he not the butler…he is responsible for taking care of the estate. Anyway how in heavens name am I supposed to know if he is single? I just met him. You know I am still trying to get over the whole Scott debacle."

Emma laughed. "Well, you are just going to have to do what feels natural. Did you take the lingerie we bought from Macy's last week? One look at you wearing that and the guy will cave."

Amanda scooted off the toilet. "Emma, are you serious? I am not freeloading in this billion-dollar estate looking for a date. Maybe I should let you face this guy Hamilton yourself. You are really not taking this seriously."

"Geez, take it easy. Don't bail on me now. Anyways, what is wrong with wanting you to have some fun? I have a good feeling about this mystery butler. I will pray for you."

Emma hung up the phone.

Amanda would have thrown the iPhone in the toilet if it wasn't her favorite gadget. Determined to leave killing her best friend for another day, the huge bathtub beckoned her gaze. Without hesitation, she removed her last stitch of clothing. She lifted her long auburn hair and set it to the side and leaned back in the tub. The warm water felt very soothing. *What a situation this is.*

From the angle of the tub, she could see out the window and downstairs. Amanda let herself rest for a while, and the strange, liberating feeling of being somewhere completely unexpected, completely new seemed to take hold. Marcus Davidson's physique stuck in her imagination, and she remembered the smile he had given her. Amanda was very self-conscious about her voluptuous body, but the way he had been looking at her was almost…possessive. She was probably mistaken but a harmless fantasy never hurt anyone.

Her hand slipped under the water and between her legs. She imagined Marcus lying on the white cotton sheets in the guesthouse, his body long and lean, feeling toned and supple in the summer night air. She could provide him with a treat in the middle of the night, take his half awaken dick and put it in her mouth, taste the salty skin and move her mouth up and down, silently, until he murmured with pleasure as he slept. Then she could work it with her hand and make it hard. He would wake up and blink with a big smile on his face. Then Amanda would hold on to him with one hand while she straddled him in the night air—

The guesthouse cordless phone rang. Amanda jumped in surprise making a splash of water go over the tub. *Great.* She'd soaked her Marlboro Menthols.

The call was from the main house. A friendly woman's voice told her that Marcus had left to meet her for dinner at the stables. Amanda thanked her for the call and grabbed a towel.

***

MARCUS DAVIDSON was having a hard time, *literally*, focusing on the task at hand. And the task at hand was showing Amanda Cardwell a good time. Unfortunately, his dick had its own ideas of what it meant to "have a good time."

"Look, over the hill. Can you see the horses?" Marcus walked Amanda down a pathway back behind the guesthouse. The main house loomed large behind them, with its epic roof structures and sheer size.

"I didn't see that there was a barn when I first arrived!"

15

Amanda loved horses. Although she hadn't had the opportunity to ride in years, this was a delightful surprise.

Marcus was enthralled. The way her face lit up made her beauty irresistible. Keeping his hands off of her for the next couple of days would prove to be a challenge.

Taking her hand, he tried to ignore the tendril of awareness between them as he walked her down to the large red barn. Two older horses poked their heads out and casually swayed their tails.

"This is Enya, and this is Lister." Marcus pulled a bag of vegetables from his rucksack. "Here, why don't you feed them a treat?" *Give me some time to get this raging erection under control.*

Amanda laughed at Enya who licked her hand gently as she took a carrot. She rubbed her mane.

"Would you like to go ride them? I can get them saddled in no time."

"Oh, I don't know. It's getting late." She eyed the horses thoughtfully.

"Nonsense, it's the perfect time for a ride."

CHAPTER 4

Having retrieved the saddles and gotten his horse ready, Marcus stepped forward to saddle Enya. Somehow he was only a breath length away from Amanda.

He felt the heat of her skin enveloping him. A cool breeze swept across the lawn, lifting her red curls and tossing the soft strands across his bare arms. Then her hand brushed his. He though his tenuous hold on propriety was about to falter.

He yearned to close his eyes for a brief moment, and savor her softness. Abruptly he stepped back from her.

Marcus finished setting up the saddle and unbridled the first horse. In one fell swoop he effortlessly lifted her into the seat as if she was as light as a feather.

"Ok, let's get going!" He spurred his horse and they began to trot towards the waterfront along a walking trail.

As she rode on the horse next to him, his gaze was irresistibly drawn to her. From the very first moment, he had known he wanted her. He couldn't help but notice her creamy white breasts and his expression darkened. What did *she* think of *him*?

The ride lasted about 45 minutes, and Amanda got to travel along the water for almost the entire perimeter of the estate. Marcus kept her bridle in one hand. Amanda hadn't ridden in years. She felt like a novice again. But Marcus was in complete control of both animals. She marveled at the fun she was having. She patted the horse as it went. It was as if the old girl knew Amanda was tentative so she went extra easy.

They rode mostly in silence, each puzzled by the crazy instant attraction they had. Before long, the ride had come to an end. They returned after settling the horses and Marcus walked her to the guesthouse.

"I've had an eventful day so far, Marcus. Thank you for all of this. I mean it." She was breathtaking underneath the porch, with the sunlight framing her angelic features. Marcus looked at her with an impenetrable expression. She smiled and his shaft hardened. He nearly reached out to caress her face. *I can't do this, not now.*

"The day isn't over yet. We still have a dinner date at 6 p.m." Giving up all pretenses he turned on his heel and walked away before she got an eyeful of his hard erection.

***

ABOUT AN HOUR later, they assembled at the dock gazebo to eat. The sun was beginning to set. It had been a beautiful day. For dinner, Marcus unveiled a picnic basket. Amanda half expected a red and white-checkered towel in the basket, but instead it was boxes of takeout. It was takeout from Bonefish, the upscale seafood eatery. Amanda smiled; she was so hungry she would have gladly eaten anything at this point. They ate shark, perfectly cooked, in a white sauce, still warm, and sprayed with pepper. Arrayed around the table were some bottles of white wine and ice water.

"Doesn't the mighty Grant Hamilton have a full kitchen to cook for him?"

"Yes he does, but most of the staff is away this weekend. Besides the odd gardener or two, you won't see many people."

"I must admit I am curious about Grant err — has he spoken about me at all?" She twirled her fork, attempting to appear cool and nonchalant.

Marcus chewed thoughtfully before he spoke.

"Mr. Hamilton is a private man. He mentioned that the first time he saw you was on a web camera, and he hasn't stopped thinking about you since." His eyes darkened as he gazed at her intensely. "He was excited, of that there was—" he let his gaze caress her sensual features, "—no doubt." The intensity of his gaze had her nipples hardening at the thought of him licking them.

"But tell me about you now, Emma. I know that you just came from Philadelphia." He folded his napkin and put it on his lap. "What is it you do in Philadelphia?"

Amanda blanched. Whose story should she tell? If she talked about her life as a scientist, it would definitely be a sharp contrast to Emma's prior conversations. But if she talked about Emma, she could talk about working at the Gentleman's Night Club and such, but she didn't think she could pull it off.

"Wouldn't you like to know?" she smiled. "I am career girl, I like the science field. I am a lab chemist, well, pharmaceutical research and development. I bet you didn't know that—"she spilled her wine glass on the fish. "Whoops! Look at me." Embarrassed now, she could feel a flush. She continued to babble as she tidied up her mess. "There's a lot going on the fields of biotechnology now. I, err, read the newspapers. Like Forbes Magazine, they say that there could be a cure for some cancers in the next 10 years."

The stress of this charade was becoming too much. With horror, Amanda thought she might burst out in tears. *Why am I being such a baby?*

"Well, yes, DNA sequencing is coming of age. They can tell what treatments your DNA is going to respond to and they can tailor a treatment plan to an individual."

She had a bite of a Bang Bang Shrimp. "They can take your blood out of your body, and then blast it with stem cells, so they can give you a much higher dose of chemotherapy. Then they put your blood back in your body, it's like being reborn with a new immune system."

Marcus was listening intently. He noticed her hand shaking slightly and suddenly put his hand on top of hers. His thumb started slowly caressing her pulse.

"You seem nervous?"

"It's just the jitters I guess. I suppose I am nervous about meeting Mr. Hamilton," Amanda blurted out. She couldn't think properly because his hand was sending delicious tendrils of desire straight to her vagina. Marcus was staring at her intensely. They were sitting so close she could smell his delicious aftershave mixed with 100% hunk. *This is crazy. I haven't been this horny since I was a teenager.*

Amanda's mouth felt like dried up parchment and she licked her lips. Although she didn't mean to be sensual or for this to be an invitation, Marcus's eyes darkened visibly and there could be no doubt about the desire emanating from his dark stare. *OMG I think this gorgeous guy wants me. Can't go there Amanda* she thought to herself. *I might be a fake mail-order bride but I have no intention of cheating on my fake fiancé!*

"Eh, excuse me; I have to go to the ladies room."

***

LOCKED IN THE POSH downstairs WC or whatever you would call a water closet that is the size of a flat, Amanda sat down on the chaise long. *Who in heavens name has a reclining chair in a toilet?*

She knew it was ridiculous to run to the loo just to get away from a guy, but she didn't care. He was stealing her breath away. Her nipples were hard as pebbles and her panties were starting to become soaking wet with need. Looking around to make sure she was alone she put her finger down her briefs. Her clit was so moisturized her finger slipped straight into her vagina.

Her breath caught in her throat as she swiftly diddled herself. It felt so good her knees started shaking, while a knot of pleasure coiled tighter in her stomach. She strangled another moan in her throat as she reached up to curl her fingers against the supple curve of her own breast, squeezing lightly, tugging at those super-sensitive nipples. Now that she had started she didn't want to stop until she came. She was so close; she just needed another push, just a nudge to tip her over the edge.

"I want you to fuck me Marcus." The words surprised her, the simple unpolished hunger of them. "Fuck me Marcus," she breathed hotly, her head rolling back as she felt the quivering overtake her. "Please fuck me," she repeated in an unbroken whispered chant as her orgasm washed over her in a wave of intense pleasure. She had to press her fingers into her mouth to muffle her moans. She lay there panting and breathing hard for a few moments. She couldn't control the trembling from the aftershocks that left her body flush and satiated.

Had she just masturbated herself to an orgasm in a public place? The thought seemed ludicrous until she saw her own glistening wetness smeared all over her fingers. She had never been able to make herself come this fast. *All this pussy juice because of a hot look from Marcus Davidson?* She scrambled to her feet quickly. Oh God! Was that a wet spot on the chaise long? Damn! Had the bathroom attendant heard her?

These places always had someone lurking around. The thought made her cringe. She was adventurous but she would not live down the shame of someone knowing what she had just done. She put her ear against the door to hear if someone was out there. Nope, the coast seemed clear. Amanda gave a quiet breath of gratitude to whichever Saint it was who looked over public masturbators.

She adjusted her panties and walked out of the bathroom straight into Marcus Davidson.

"I wondered where you had gone to. Is everything alright?"

"Yes, sorry I needed to take a breather. Too much wine."

"Well, I will leave you to it. I will see you later for our midnight boat tour." He took her hand and brushed his hot lips over it. Suddenly his eyes were alight with desire.

"Yes, I will leave you to it indeed." It was only on her way to her room for a quick change that she realized the hand he had kissed was the one still smeared with her pussy juices. *Is it possible to die of embarrassment?*

CHAPTER 5

Boats were moving slowly in the water, and patio lanterns along the dock shone colored circles in the dark blue water.

"I have organized for us to take the estate yacht out tonight. I thought we could do a circle around the bay.

"Yes, it's so beautiful here, I'd like that."

Amanda was a little tipsy getting up the gang plank. They had, had drinks even before setting out to the boat. She focused hard so she didn't trip and end up in the drink. Marcus put one hand in hers, and another on her back. She could feel the heat emanating from his touch. He traced his hand tantalizingly down her back, his caress a promise of delights to come. Amanda shivered with anticipation. Being a big curvy girl she had never met a man that made her feel this delicate, precious, and petit. Marcus Davidson was one in a million.

Oh for God's sake, you are an impostor at a billionaire's mansion, keep this daydreaming up and you will end up being fucked by the groundskeeper. Determined she decided to ignore the caress and moved towards one of the deck chairs. Marcus busied himself with unhooking the vessel.

Once the boat left the dock, they listened to some music above deck. Gun's N Roses *November Rain* was on and Amanda swayed to the music with her wine glass half full.

The air was heavy with unspoken tension and desire. Why had Marcus brought her out here? He was currently busy behind the wheel, and gunned the motor for a minute or two. When he was satisfied they were in a good spot, he reached for the anchor release. Amanda felt the boat come to an abrupt stop in the water; she lost her balance and gravity pushed her directly into Marcus' lap.

"Marcus, did you do that on purpose?" she laughed breathlessly, and threw her arms around him.

"No, I've been drinking. Shame on me. You never should drink and drive."

"It's totally true, *you shouldn't.* Captain, you are relieved of duty." She crossed her leg over his. She could smell *L'Homme* by Jean-Paul Gaultier mixed with the musky scent of him, it was enticing. *What the hell am I doing?* All thoughts of Scott, her philandering ex-lover had evaporated from her mind.

"You know all the wealth here, all the beauty of this home. It's really, really great. But I would never want to marry a man for money."

"Aren't you the mail-order bride?" Marcus looked bemused.

"Well, yes, well, no, I mean— oh, it's really complicated." She didn't want him to think she was superficial or fickle. But how could she make him understand without telling him the truth?

"What I mean to say was that what I want in life is a man I

can trust. Someone to share life's highs and lows with. Someone I can completely be myself with." *And you might just be that someone.*

Amanda was blazing hot from the day spent in the sun. The wine did not help things. Marcus ran his finger up her arm, and it felt like a lightning bolt. Sitting on his lap, she could feel him underneath her bottom. The bulge she was sitting on was growing bigger. Oh my God, he's hard! She thought. *This is about to get complicated.*

Marcus looked on, silently appraising her. His eyes settled on her breasts again. He knew she felt his cock swelling hard. For a moment he luxuriated in the image of her. Slowly he turned her torso towards him. He ached to explore the softness of her ample breasts up close. His hands fisted, and he forced his mind to retreat from thoughts of taking her then and there, foreplay be damned.

His dark eyes locked with hers.

"You know Emma, Mr. Hamilton expects his mail-order bride to be waiting for him when he returns, and in good condition. What do you think he would say if he found out I had fucked you?" He hoped against his better judgment that his crude words would get her off his lap. He didn't have the strength to push her away.

Instead of answering, she started lightly grinding her hips against his bulge. Her creamy breasts were bouncing slowly back and forth under his nose. His shaft grew impossibly harder.

Marcus growled low in his throat "But then, wouldn't Mr. Hamilton want to know what you feel like, what you taste like..." he was murmuring now, caressing one of her peaks with his hand. She rubbed her breasts up against his hand, and with a deft motion he had freed the strap of her dress. One of her large breasts was loose, he marveled for a moment, and then kissed it softly, raining little flicks of his tongue against her nipple. His cock, impossibly hard was rubbing against her thigh.

Amanda could feel Marcus's heart pounding, as his chest pressed against hers nearly in time to the powerful throbbing between her legs. The sensation of his hand on her bare skin was setting her on fire. All the reasons why she shouldn't be doing this flashed through her mind.

They had just met. She was supposed to be someone else's bride. Nothing worked, she couldn't restrain herself. Her sexual fantasy from earlier in the day flashed before her eyes.

She had never known such sexual power. This beautiful, gorgeous specimen of a man was groaning because of her. Her very presence was making him rock hard. She wanted— no needed to soothe his throbbing ache. Her hands moved down to Marcus's canvas pants, and she almost unbuttoned him with one snap.

The zipper came down easy, and she realized miraculously that she was still holding her wine glass with the other hand. She set it down, and moved her hand down between his legs. His cock was straight up against his stomach, and she lifted his shorts down just a bit and had him in her hand.

Marcus knew that if he let her, she was about to give him the tongue lashing he had been longing for. The thought of her luscious moist lips encircling his hard shaft almost had him undone. But this was not what he wanted for their first time. There would be plenty of time to sample her oral pleasuring later.

"Take off your panties." His order came out as a growl.

"What?" Amanda thought she might have misheard. She was

still heady from the discovery that she could bring this man to his knees.

"You've been a very bad girl Amanda. Masturbating in public tsk, tsk."

"But I—" Amanda didn't get a word in.

"Don't lie to me. I caught the scent of your creamy fluids when I kissed your hand earlier. The thought of what you were up to in the water closet has kept me hard all evening."

Terribly ashamed Amanda tried to look anywhere but at Marcus. Her cheeks were aflame and now matched the fiery red of her hair. As she stared resolutely at her feet, Marcus put the tip of his finger under her chin and lifted her face towards him. The desire that burned in his eyes was all the encouragement Amanda needed. Unable and unwilling to deny him, she rose from his lap. Extremely self-conscious of how vulnerable she was she nonetheless lifted up her dress skirt and pulled down her panties. Shyly she stepped out of them, now standing before him with no underwear.

She looked more sexy than Venus and sensual as hell. Marcus's good intentions all went out the window. Like a starving man at a buffet he had to restrain himself from devouring her. As he stalked up to her she took a nervous step backward until she was backed against the railing. Gently he spun her around. Her creamy neck called to him as he inhaled her intoxicating scent. As he nibbled his way down to her shoulder the dark desires driving him had him roughly lift her dress up. Her bare, creamy, round bottom looked delectable in the moonlight. He put his nose up to the dip at the bottom of her spine, breathed in deeply, and exhaled. He breathed in again, and then shocked her by slapping her on the rump, hard.

Marcus put both of his strong hands around Amanda's waist, and lifted her delicious ass towards him. His knowing hand moved with the precision of a machinist, to find her moist, aching clit. Automatically her legs parted. He let his finger slide along her cleft. She was perfect, hot, and dripping. His thumb now shaking pressed into her sweet spot.

"Yes," she gasped her eyes closed, as she clung to the railing in front of her.

"So beautiful, so beautiful", he murmured, breathing in her smell. Marcus knelt down on the deck and Amanda stuck her rear out, arching her back. Her head was lowered against the railing as she moaned. Marcus inserted one chunky finger into her wet pussy. The moaning was replaced by gasps of pleasure. Marcus nuzzled his nose against her backside, breathing in deeply, tracing his lips across the skin. He only meant to ease one finger in, to get a quick taste of her, and then walk away. But she was so hot and tight. Helpless against the scent of her desire and his own raging erection – he sank a second finger in.

"Yes," she moaned with abandon.

He rained little kisses against her buttocks as his fingers worked on driving her wild. As she pushed back against his digits desperate for even more, Marcus was unable to resist the allure of her wanton sighs. Her scent had his hormones raging. He hastily got up and pulled his pants off. He was not going to spill his seed on the floor like an untrained schoolboy. But if he didn't penetrate her soon, he might just do that.

Trembling he took a hold of his hard shaft guiding it against her moist entrance. She gasped at the feel of him. He somehow found the strength to not instantly pound in her. Instead he used his hard cock to massage her softness. His cock reminding her, he was all man and she was all woman. He was hard as steel and thick. He started pushing slowly. His cock was stretching her deliciously wide open. He let her feel his slow but unyielding possession of her. He spread her round rear cheeks to make sure she would receive the full measure of him. With his cock finally inside her all the way to the hilt, he came undone. Her tight heat was more than any man could bear. He started thrusting into her in hard, deep strokes.

He held her torso down almost against the wood of the railing, and pushed her ass up further so he could penetrate even deeper between her bouncy passage. Her moaning grew louder as his strokes moved faster. His finger played up and down against her clitoris, and she could feel her orgasm building.

He tried to hold back, but it was futile. Amanda's ass bucked a little, she looked backward, her eyes hooded with pleasure. Their gaze locked. Releasing himself deep inside her became the only thought on his mind. Marcus fucked her even harder, with shortened strokes, like a madman. *Oh delicious possession.*

Then he burst inside her. His orgasm sailed her off the cliff at the same time, and her pussy pulsed in time with his spurting cock. Marcus shuddered a few more times, and then pulled his cock out. They were spent. Amanda could barely stand. Exhausted, she sat back down.

"Whoa." She tried to catch her breath. "Marcus. That was— I've never…" Amanda Cardwell, Senior Lab Chemist and Senior Loser in Love was lost for words. She wasn't the kind of girl to have a one night stand even during her party years. It took more than a pretty smile, but somehow Marcus had broken through all those inhibitions and made her want him in a way no other man ever had. Then reality hit her. What must he think of her? He couldn't hold her in high regard, especially if he thought she was Emma. The glowing haze of their lovemaking turned cold. She didn't want him to be sleeping with Emma. She wanted him to know he was with Amanda.

There was no such thing as love at first sight. It was because of stupid ideas like that, that she had ended up dating Scott, the two timing bastard. But even as she chided herself she knew to do what they had just done, with no protection on top of everything else her feelings for him were more than just physical. She needed to tell him the truth before it went too far.

"Marcus, there's something I need to tell you. I am not who you think I am. My name is not Emma Baker, it's Amanda Cardwell."

CHAPTER 6

Amanda woke up the next morning back at the guesthouse. The other side of the bed was empty, Marcus hadn't stayed. At some point after her amazing orgasm she'd confessed everything to him on their way back to the manor. Marcus hadn't said a word. He had just brought her home, tucked her in, and said they would talk about it tomorrow.

She looked around her room and saw her sandals and dress piled neatly on the table. There was a note next to it. She flipped it over and was disappointed; it was merely the receipt from Bonefish.

She looked tentatively at the home security panel. Should she call Marcus? *No, don't be crazy. The guy is probably freaked out; he just banged his boss' fake bride.*

Amanda had a niggling sensation that something was wrong. *Things are getting way too complicated.*

Suddenly, it dawned on her what it was. *He never kissed me.*

In the heat of the moment she hadn't noticed, but there it was. It was irrefutable evidence that whilst she had been making love, he clearly was just having a fuck. How had she missed it? She felt like crying. *They hadn't kissed.* In a panic, she pressed the connect button on the security touch screen.

The screen lit up and a lady dressed in business attire looked disapprovingly at Amanda.

"Can I help you?" she said flatly.

"I'm sorry to be disturbing you this early. I am looking for Marcus, is he there? "

The woman looked mildly irritated. "Marcus is not working today. He's off."

"Oh, ok — well, thank you..." Amanda tried to sound friendly but the woman hung up the video call. Or at least, the picture went black. She could hear the lady muttering something to another woman. They were cursing in Spanish.

"I heard Master Hamilton got himself a mail-order bride, one of those sexy leggy blonde ones. Apparently they sent him some voluptuous replacement. He has her up in the guesthouse."

"Mariah says she thinks they spent the night together. Can you imagine? They have only known each other for 24 hours. My lord, what have we come to here? This place is turning into a bordello."

Another voice said something in Spanish that sounded even more disapproving.

Amanda was mortified. She clicked on the power button of her screen, killing the inadvertent audio playback. She sat down on the bed, stunned.

Her secret was out! Marcus must have told the staff. Amanda felt betrayed and confused. He didn't have to spread it around.

Clearly to him last night had been a one-time thing, since he had rushed off to reveal her secret. She felt ashamed, but mostly angry.

Amanda knew she had to leave now before Hamilton came home, or before the situation got any worse. She hurriedly gathered her belongings. She called Emma four or five times, but no answer.

Amanda took one last look at the guesthouse. She didn't understand why, but she felt like crying her eyes out.

Like some perp walk of shame back in college, Amanda kept her head down, her carry-on luggage trailing behind her, a proverbial tail.

Thankfully, no one was out and about. The sun was coming up now, another endlessly sunny day in Florida. There were a few clouds in the sky to the north. Along the walkway, birds were chirping in the grass, which was cut immaculately. She walked in the shadow of the main house, up the driveway. Her thoughts were elsewhere. *He didn't kiss me.*

After a few minutes' walk, she made her way to the front gate. As soon as she left the property she would begin to feel better, she told herself. She'd check into the Embassy Suites and burn two days at Disneyland, or sit alone in the room and drink. Amanda felt tears coming on. She hadn't expected to meet someone like Marcus. She didn't understand why his opinion mattered so much to her. *He didn't kiss me.*

At the front gate, just a few hundred feet from being outside, a top of the line Lexus sat idling in the driveway. It was black, with tinted windows, and 18 inch rims. Several helpers were moving luggage off the car. Suddenly, Amanda's heart dropped. A man was getting out of the car. His black leather loafer touched the ground. *Oh God. It must be Hamilton.*

She stood still for a moment. There was time enough to leave the place and never face this man; but she thought about Emma, the dowry, and all that had happened up to this point.

Amanda knew that she needed to face the music, and to set things right. Whatever happened next, she would take it stoically. She would offer to pay for food and amenities that had been offered. Hamilton would cancel the wedding and that would be the end of it.

Amanda approached the car, with a steely resolve.

The passenger side door opened. A man with a suit stepped out, directing the help with a finger point. He turned around and Amanda was directly in front of him.

"You're up early," the man said.

Marcus, with Gucci sunglasses on, stepped towards Amanda and caught her as she fainted.

CHAPTER 7

Billionaire Tycoon Grant Hamilton stared down at the woman sleeping atop of his white, Egyptian cotton bed linens. Fiery, red hair tousled around a sensual face, long lashes casting shadows over rosy cheeks. Her hands rested between her creamy curvy legs, partially covering her half naked, luscious body. Soon to be his wife.

Maybe.
Probably
Hopefully…

Her body…her body was making him sweat. Those perfectly made for sin curves. His shaft hardened.

She was just the way he liked his women, heaving bosom and a bottom a man could grab a hold of. One look and a man knew she would be a firecracker when her passions were unleashed.

Yesterday had been more than enough proof of that.

From the very first moment he saw her in Emma's summer holiday video clips he had been obsessed with getting to know her. Her plump cherry red lips had haunted his dreams. A man could die in peace knowing pleasure from those lips.

When Emma had cancelled their arrangement it had suited him perfectly. This was an opportunity for him to convince her to send her friend as a replacement. At first she had balked at the idea, until he had convinced her that Amanda would be perfectly safe.

Seeing her for the first time, looking like a walking hot sex dream had him almost undone. The last time he had been this out of control was when he had his first wet dream at the age of 14. He kept repeating to himself – *whatever you do, don't get hard.* Easier said than done.

Up close and personal she hadn't been as perfect as he had thought. *She'd been even better.* A smattering of freckles dotted her sweetly sloped nose. Her lace balconette brazier exposed mounds of soft female flesh. He remembered their red hot sex session the night before and felt himself hardening again.

How was she going to react now that she had found out he was a billionaire? That he had been deceiving her all along. Would she stomp off, or was there even a remote chance that she would give this a go?

Unfortunately for her he had no intentions of taking any chances. He was as ruthless in love, as in business. He was not known for taking no for an answer.

***

AMANDA WOKE UP disorientated. Her first sight was Marcus looking inquisitively at her. Why was he looking so serious? Then it hit her. This wasn't Marcus; this was Grant Hamilton, tycoon, billionaire, and playboy. He had played her for a fool, right from the start. She had responded by fainting like a 15 year old school girl. She could feel her face heating up from the embarrassment of it all. She had practically thrown herself at him. When she thought about how easily she had succumbed to his charms she felt mortified. To think she actually once thought she might be falling in love with him. *What a fool I am, yet another mistake.*

The silence was unbearable. It was pregnant with unspoken accusations and desire.

"Right, if you could get out of my room, I will gather my things and be leaving shortly." The tart statement was delivered in a dry voice.

"Where do you think you are going?"

"Home. Clearly you've had your laugh and more," her thoughts flashed to his hard possession of her body on the boat. "I will be on my way."

"You will do no such thing. I haven't finished with you." Grant's steel gaze had her pinned to the bed. *What in heaven's name was he talking about? Was he a secret deranged killer?*

"Listen, I don't know what kind of women you have been hanging around with, but this isn't the middle ages and fucking me doesn't give you the right to tell me what to do." Amanda hoisted herself up from the bed, and then she realized she was only in her underwear, grabbed the sheet, tangled herself up in her haste and fell on her face.

She had never felt so mortified in her life. She was definitely on a darn roll! *Good thing this carpet is nice and soft.*

Grant rushed to her side "Are you alright?"

Despite his earlier harsh words, concern was etched all over his face. The special, delicious fragrance that was uniquely him was assaulting her weakened defenses.

"I am fine." Amanda pulled herself up and started looking for her clothes. Why had he undressed her? What kind of madhouse was she in?

"Calm down. You are perfectly safe. The same cannot be said for your friend Emma." Amanda stopped straight in her track. What did he mean?

"You confessed to me yourself yesterday that you are not Emma Baker. You are well aware that Emma is under a contractual obligation to become my bride or return the dowry down payment she received. Having sent you in her place I can only assume that she has no intention to keep to our agreement. Clearly I will have to contact my lawyers."

"But you're a billionaire; $50,000 is pocket change to you." Amanda protested.

"I paid a significant sum of money for a mail-order bride," Grant continued, as if she hadn't uttered a word.

"Preparations have been made, expectations have been set. All of society knows I am soon to be married. I have no intention of robbing them of that assumption or inconveniencing myself by choosing another for that matter. Although you are not the one I ordered you will do." His words were delivered cold, without emotion.

"What?!" Amanda thought she must be hallucinating.

"I think you heard me the first time. Do you intend to honor Emma's contract, or should I get my lawyers to enforce the repayment of the dowry immediately? I hear prison orange is the new black." Why in heaven's name did he want her to continue with this charade? Were all rich men tightwads?

Amanda felt like the fairytale princess who just found out that Prince Charming didn't exist.

"You need to decide now. Are you going through with this or are you going to let your best friend go to jail?"

"Jail?" she whispered the word with dread.

"Yes, jail. That is what happens when you rob someone of $50,000 and can't pay it back." Grant stared at her intensely.

"It's not all bad. The contract is for two years. You will be provided with a monthly allowance and a lump sum for every child born within the marriage. Based on yesterday I would say you are not averse to fucking me, this particular clause should not be a problem."

The silence between them was heavy with apprehension. Was she prepared to give up her life and enter a loveless marriage for the next couple of years to save her friend? How far would she go? Sensing her indecision Grant walked up to her and gently caressed her cheek.

"Surely the prospect of being married to me isn't that horrendous?"

It wasn't. Last night's lovemaking flashed before her eyes. The memory of his throbbing cock pounding into her, made her weak at the knees with desire.

In the end making the decision wasn't that hard after all. The truth was quite simple, she wanted to know his full possession, never mind the reason for their liaison.

"I… Eh, yes," Amanda stuttered. "I mean, are you quite sure? I know a couple of friends who would marry you in a heartbeat." *What am I saying? I want him for myself.*

"Interesting, I don't think I need any other brides," Grant said casually. "Our engagement party is tomorrow. Since I only organized it this morning, you won't have the opportunity to meet my family. But we will have another party at my parents' house next month."

"Sorry? Did you say engagement party?" This was all going way too fast. Meeting his friends and then his family! She had just agreed to be his mail-order bride, 10 seconds ago. He was throwing her into the deep end.

"I bought you a suitable dress. You will find it on your dresser." Grant told her coldly and walked away.

Amanda's mind was racing. He must be kidding. Maybe he would change his mind once he saw her big bosom. Men like him tended to prefer flat chested, anorexic girls. Somehow that did not calm the rolling sensation of apprehension in her stomach. *Wait a minute; he's already seen me naked!*

CHAPTER 8

A manda Hamilton. *Amanda Hamilton*...She better get used to that name. The engagement party had already started. She could hear music and laughter from downstairs, and she was still in the bedroom trying to gather her courage. Having tried Emma's number a million times since yesterday, she had concluded she was on her own. No time to change her mind.

At least the dress Grant had bought for her made her feel like a Goddess. It was a shimmering gold gown that complemented her complexion. The V-neck had an underlining supporting structure that not only put her breast on display but held them there defying gravity. The hem hugged her round bottom in a way that would have made even J-Lo jealous. Thank God it had a supporting panel around her waist to flatten her curvy tummy. *Tucked in and in control. You can do this.*

"Are you ready to go downstairs?" Grant was standing by the door, looking devastatingly handsome in his black dinner suit.

"I bought you a ring." He took a blue box out of his pocket and opened it to display the most gorgeous green emerald solitaire she had ever seen.

"It wouldn't do if my bride to be was running around without an engagement ring. It is green to match your eyes."

Amanda watched him put it on her finger and felt like a condemned prisoner. *How can he be so romantic and so cold all at the same time?* To his credit, he allowed her a few minutes to reconcile with her pending fate. However mere minutes wouldn't be enough. She doubted that months or years could make this event seem less surreal. Things like this did not happen to plump ex-party girls from Philly.

***

THE WOMEN WERE STARING at Grant, like he was the first and last dish in a 7-course meal. Amanda had never felt so self-conscious in her life. A particularly stunning long legged blonde started walking towards them. She looked like a cross between Cameron Diaz and Jessica Biel.

"Grant, darling. Long time no see," the blonde purred. She pointedly ignored Amanda and laced herself around Grant's arm.

"We missed you in the Hamptons this spring. Ben has been hankering to go to Aspen in the next couple of weeks. Are you game?" Grant turned towards Amanda.

"Natasha, meet my fiancée Amanda Cardwell."

"Yes… interesting."

Amanda took a deep breath. *Best to get this over and done with.*

"Nice to meet you, Natasha. I hope we can become friends."

Natasha pointedly continued to ignore her. Amanda could

vaguely hear the conversation she was having with Grant. She was mortified by the whole situation. Yesterday had been a wonderful fairytale adventure, which was now clearly at an end. Somewhere deep inside her she had to admit that being the center of this man's world for however short a time had been a heady experience.

"Will you excuse us," she heard Grant say. "My fiancée and I need to mingle."

"Oh," Natasha protested looking curiously at Amanda.

"So it is true, you are getting married. This isn't one of your eccentric games?"

"Yes I am marrying Amanda," he said with emphasis. "She has mesmerized me as no other woman ever has." Amanda didn't know who was more surprised, her or Natasha. The woman turned around and looked at her, her facial expression clearly showed disbelief that a man like Grant would hitch his wagon to a woman like her. She walked quietly back to her table and immediately started whispering with her table companions.

***

WHEN THE PARTY was in full swing. Amanda finally found a quiet corner to hide away from all the prying eyes.

"Would you have believed it, if you hadn't seen it for yourself?"

"Grant Hamilton engaged to a fat girl. What was he thinking? I am sure this is a scheme cooked up by that Grandmother of his. She was always a busybody."

"Well, this engagement party doesn't mean anything. Natasha is at this very moment having a quiet heart to heart with Grant.

43

Clearly he never got over her breaking their engagement two months ago. This hair brain scheme is obviously his way of trying to make her jealous."

He had proposed to somebody else recently? Looking at the myriad faces of the people in the ballroom Amanda felt devastated. This party was turning out to be a trial by fire. Surely she must have heard wrong. She didn't want to enter a marriage of convenience where she would be made a laughing stock across the country. Where was Grant? *I am probably over reacting. The man I spent the day with would not marry one woman just to have another as his mistress.*

Frantically searching for her fiancé she finally heard his voice coming through the door of one of the spare bedrooms. Who was he talking to?

Natasha was tangling her hands through Grant's hair.

"Darling, it's been a while. If I would have known that your reaction to the refusal of my marriage proposal would be this ludicrous engagement to a no-body I would have said yes."

"Natasha we are not having this conversation." *Why didn't he tell her it wasn't ludicrous and she wasn't a nobody?*

"So I refused to get pregnant straight away. That was an issue we could have negotiated on. Besides, how do you know your new fiancée is even fertile?"

"She has childbearing hips."

"You mean she has a fat ass?"

Unable to hear any more disparaging remarks about her body, Amanda spun on her heel bumping into a side ornament on her headlong dash back to her room. He just wanted to get her pregnant. *I am not going to cry.*

***

GRANT TURNED AROUND just in time to see the hem of his fiancée's dress dash past a corner. Amanda looked upset. *Damn.*

"Natasha I don't have time for your silly little games. You know very well why we broke up."

"Sure I do. You're a pervert. You are lucky I haven't let half the world know."

"Let me be very clear. If I hear one more disparaging word about my future bride or find out you have been spreading rumors about me, I will make sure I use my considerable wealth and business contacts to strip your father of your entire fortune leaving you destitute. I wonder how many men you will be able to attract then."

With those final words he spun around and with brisk steps went to find his mail-order bride. Had he lingered and turned around, he would have been disturbed to see Natasha's evil smirk as she watched him walk away.

CHAPTER 9

His gaze held hers.

"Why did you run off?" Grant asked Amanda, puzzled.

"I didn't know you needed me to stay. Clearly you and your mistress had everything in hand."

"Mistress?"

"Don't play innocent with me. I could see how you were looking at each other." Irritated Amanda stomped off to her wardrobe and started removing her jewelry.

"What is it that you think you know?"

"Don't treat me like an idiot Grant. Clearly you were after a woman to carry your children, whilst you have your mistress on the side."

Grant watched as Amanda paced the room. His need to soothe her was overshadowed by his anger that she thought so little of him. Had she learnt nothing over the last two days? If she thought she could leave she was about to learn how wrong she was.

"I think we need to establish some boundaries, and this as

good a time to start as any." Grant's voice brokered no argument.

"I paid for a mail-order bride," he continued. "You agreed to the arrangement. I intend to hold you to that. I mean to have a normal marriage with all that that entails. Including claiming *my marital rights* in bed. Yesterday I went easy on you." His words were delivered dead calm.

"I want to make sure we are compatible in every way," he continued while removing his tie then his jacket.

"I have particular tastes, so let's see if you can satisfy them." He started unbuttoning his shirt.

"Take off your clothes."

"What?" Amanda thought she might have misheard.

"I have particular tastes. I like administering sexual punishment. I need to know if you can take it. Take all I have to give before this goes any further." Never had Grant said these words to another, but his need to possess her heart and soul, went beyond the shame he felt about his dark desires.

Surely he didn't mean… Amanda, made breathless by his confession, swallowed her next words. *What did he mean by sexual punishment?*

Although the mere mention of marital sex had her getting all hot and bothered, Amanda was confused about what to do. She would have slept with him without the engagement or the threat of imprisonment of her friend hanging over her head *(what girl wouldn't)*, but she wasn't sure she could handle whatever he was about to dish out. The butterflies in her stomach had still not subsided. It was clear from the look in Grant's eyes there would be no denying him.

"The choice is yours. Either you do as I ask or you walk away. Make your choice. But know this, *I yearn to bury myself deep inside you.*"

Grant looked at her, their gaze locked and held. Amanda forgot to breathe, to think, to move. The intensity of his emotions was like a magnet. Yesterday everything had been so easy. He was just a man, she was just a girl. Today she was the mail-order bride. To be surveyed and judged on her beauty, wit, and desirability.

In the end, making the choice to surrender to whatever sexual play he had in mind wasn't that hard after all. She was already weak at the knees with desire for this man. She pulled down the top of her evening gown and let it gather in a pool around her ankles.

Grant let his eyes feast on the decadent sight in front of him. Her breasts were beautifully framed by her white cotton bra. Creamy pink and delicate, they made him salivate to lavish them with his tongue. He already knew he desired her, that he wanted to savor her sweet innocence by fucking the hell out of her again, but would she be able to handle it? She might think she was experienced (so many modern women did), but he required total submission. The punishment he was about to dish out would leave both of them spent and wanting for more.

"Take your panties off. I want to see the bright red color of your pussy."

"I am not a whore for hire dammit!" Amanda was starting to regret following his initial instructions to begin with. Without preamble Grant walked up to her, put his hand down her damp cotton briefs and inserted his chunky index finger into her soaking clit. She almost purred with delight. There was no denying it. She was already wet for him; all her protests were just for show.

"Just to make sure we understand each other. During the day we are equals, but during the night you are mine. *Mine to enjoy, mine to chastise, mine to devour.*" He said all this while he continued to finger fuck her pussy with his index finger.

"You will walk out of here having enjoyed every minute of my possession." Wetness pooled between her legs and her knees started to give out. Grant swept her into his arms like she weighed nothing more than a feather, and carried her to his King size bed.

She was unprepared when his mouth captured hers. With a sigh, she parted her lips, allowing his tongue to invade her moist, warm mouth.

Grant couldn't believe his good fortune when Amanda finally surrendered to his ministrations. She tasted delicious, like sweet strawberry with a hint of lime. He could have plundered her mouth for hours, but his throbbing member was having none of it.

He stilled, mesmerized by her beauty. She lay spread out for his desires. Her flaming pubic bush, like a beacon between her legs. Carefully, he caressed her mound and using both hands proceeded to spread her vaginal lips to get a better view of her enchanting tunnel. She was exquisite, so pink and juicy. He felt a twinge of shame that he was salivating to taste her, but he wasn't going to waste this opportunity. The wonderful musky fragrance of her pussy was making him harder than he had ever been; he just had to taste her. He bent down and let his lips trace her vaginal lips. She whimpered.

Encouraged, he pressed his tongue into her entrance lapping up her juices. Amanda almost bounced off the bed, but he held her down, come hell or high water; he was going to feast on her. Insistently, repeatedly he penetrated her vagina with his tongue, in and out, in and out, until her whimpers became moans of purest pleasure.

Grant pulled back. He needed to make sure she wanted this of her own free will.

"Before you get your full treat, we need to establish some ground rules. Punishment will be dispensed frequently for bad behavior. We will be starting right now. If you are not capable of receiving your punishment like a big girl, you still have the choice to walk away. The taste of your juices on my tongue will be taken as full payment on Emma's debt and you will have no more obligations towards me."

Even as he was saying the words Grant thought *Am I crazy, I don't want to let her go.* He waited in silence. The swelling bulge in the front of his dinner suit pants left no doubt about how the punishment would end.

Amanda couldn't believe he was giving her a choice this late in the game. She gulped; he wasn't really going to spank her was he? She wasn't one of those girls who are into sadomasochism; but he had given her opportunity to bail and she had opted to explore the promise of desire fulfilled that lurked in his eyes.

Her nipples were hard and her vagina was throbbing from longing. Although her mind was screaming at her to walk away, the thought of his full possession of her body made her weep with need. Besides, the glimpse she had caught of his cock made her want to whimper. Who ever said size didn't matter was a fool. Just the thought of being filled to the brim with his member had her aching for his possession.

Would he respect her in the morning? Would she respect herself? Did he even still respect her? Did it matter? When all was said and done, she already knew deep inside she wanted this, whatever this was. Her response came out no louder than a whisper. "Please...don't stop."

With a twinge of regret that he had to interrupt his feast, Grant got up. This had to be done now. The problem he had had with his other lovers was not revealing his sexual desires right from the start. He was not about to make that mistake with Amanda. He only hoped this would not be the first and the last time he would taste her delicious creaminess. Locking her gaze with his he whispered hoarsely, "Come and lay down on my lap."

Her sweet hesitant sway onto his lap almost left Grant captivated. Her ass was perfection, creamy, bouncy and soft as a rose petal. Granddad always did say *there is nothing as juicy as a tender behind.* Then again he was a rich, dirty old man, Grant mused.

With her huge breasts crushed against his leg and her pert bottom up in the air he whispered, "Spread your legs." Amanda hesitantly obeyed.

When he started finger fucking her, she thought she was going to swoon, it felt so good. Wetness pooled between her legs, and she forgot about worrying about how big she was or how she must be crushing him with her weight. She had never felt so exposed and wanton in her life.

"I am now going to insert one of my toys in your cleft to ready you for your punishment," Grant whispered. His hot breath caressed her earlobe and sent tendrils of desire straight to her wet mound.

Grant's hard cock was throbbing for release and he gritted his teeth, determined to finish her punishment before spilling his seed in her delicious cave. With firmness he inserted the first vibrating ball, then the second and finally the third.

"I expect you to clench and hold these balls in your vagina, until the end of your corporal punishment session." Amanda barely managed to nod her acceptance. The pleasure that was being generated by the balls was crippling. The more she clenched her vaginal walls, the more intense the pleasure. But the only way to keep them in was to clench, she was now so wet that they would have just slid out.

Then his hand slapped her bottom.

Smack - oh my God. He was actually doing it. Spanking her like a naughty little girl.

Smack, the heat spread through her nether regions.

Smack, more heat to stoke the flames of desire.

His hand was gently rubbing the sting away; then his index was in her pussy creating delicious friction against the vibrating balls.

Smack, the heat was back, more delicious than before.

This could not be happening to her. She was an independent, self-sufficient modern- *ahhh*, he pinched her clitoris and she thought she was going to come.

Smack

The heat from her bottom mixed with the pleasure of the balls created a symphony of pleasure and pain that Amanda didn't want to stop.

Smack

"You've been a very naughty girl."

Smack

"I enjoyed eating your creamy wetness."

Smack

"Fucking you was more satisfying than any other sexual encounter I have ever had."

Smack

"Seeing your disciplined ass, makes me harder than I have ever been in my life."

Smack

"Please stop. Ahh .. oh." How was he— why was she —*ohhh*. He had followed his spanking by inserting a finger in her pussy.

The vibration of the balls where creating waves of sensation pulsing through her body.

Suddenly Grant picked her up out of his lap and positioned her on all fours. Before she could assimilate what was happening he pulled out the balls and inserted his cock in one powerful thrust into her wet pussy. *Bliss*.

He began thrusting, first slowly, then faster and faster. He was hammering inside her and she loved it. She wanted it all. The *intensity*, the *passion*. She had made this gorgeous man lose control. With his left hand he pinched her clit during one last passionate thrust. Unable to help herself she screamed her pleasure long and hard, surrendering to the sensations.

CHAPTER 10

Grant Hamilton was in love and he couldn't have been more miserable. What had he done? He hadn't had the intention of taking it quite that far. He felt overwhelmed by what had just happened. He knew women. He could figure them out in a span of a once over. So why hadn't he realized that Amanda would break down. After her orgasm he had continued fucking her in hard deep thrusts until he came deep inside her. The pleasure had been almost unbearable. The thought of possibly impregnating her made his release even sweeter. He had never experienced anything similar.

It was at that very moment he realized he was completely and utterly in love with her. But his greatest pleasure turned into his greatest shame because only then did he notice she was sobbing quietly.

Why had he made her submit to the delicious punishment he had administered? Despite the overwhelming shame, he could feel his dick stirring at the thought of their lovemaking.

For the last six years Grant Hamilton had the same recurring problem. Sex was unsatisfying. He couldn't figure it out. The women walking in and out of his bedroom were beautiful, polished, and well-bred. He liked independent women; unfortunately that independence seemed to stretch to the bedroom. He wasn't interested in being tied up or brought to heel like a lot of high power men. The women he dated were so independent they didn't want to share their lives with anyone. As if independence meant you had to be separate or in constant conflict in a relationship.

What he *wanted* was trust. A woman that would allow him to tend to her needs and trust that he would do this in a safe and loving way.

What he *needed* was submission. A woman that would allow him to express his dominant tendencies without judgment. Who would revel in and enjoy his less than vanilla flavored sex play.

What he *craved* was a companion someone to share his time, thoughts, successes, and failures with.

He thought he found that when he met Natasha. She had fooled him for quite a while. *How naive I was.*

With Amanda everything was different. He wanted to please her.

He loved the way she got happy when she was tipsy. The way her face would go fire red when she was embarrassed. The fact that she enjoyed being disciplined, he just...loved everything about her.

He needed more, his desires couldn't possibly be fulfilled until he had taken her in every way imaginable and even then, it would still not be enough. He couldn't imagine getting enough of her. But how was he going to get her to stay after all that had happened yesterday? He wanted her to want to be his forever, of her own free will. This contract marriage would mean nothing without trust. He hoped it wasn't too late to start again.

***

AMANDA CARDWELL WAS IN LOVE and she couldn't have been more miserable. She slowly opened her eyes, when she finally heard the bedroom door close. What must he be thinking of her? Sobbing like a baby over some lovemaking. She hadn't been able to help herself. In the aftermath of her orgasm, while he was still pumping into her, sending residual waves of pleasure through her entire body, she had realized she was in love.

She had also realized he didn't love her. He hadn't denied that she was just a means to acquire an heir to his fortune. Even worse, his sexual dominance of her meant they would never be equal. He had relished his possession, and she had craved the submission. *I cannot stay.*

Quietly she pulled her clothes on, threw the bare essentials into her totem bag and walked briskly out the front door.

"Could I possibly trouble you to drive me to the nearest hotel?"

"I am sorry miss; Mr. Grant has asked that no-one leave the manor today."

"Do you know where I can get a cab?"

"I am very sorry; he specifically asked that you not leave the villa until he has had a chance to speak to you. Maybe we could call him?"

"No— thanks I will wait." *I have to get out of here. If I don't leave now, I will never get away.* Amanda suddenly remembered the horses. She wasn't a horse woman, but if she could just hold on long enough surely she could get to the manor house in the neighboring estate and ask for assistance. *I cannot stay.* As she clung on to Enya for dear life she failed to notice the pothole they were headed straight for. When the mare stopped abruptly she was caught completely off guard and went flying.

***

AMANDA WOKE UP DISORIENTATED. Her head was pounding like she had just spent seven nights partying with zero recovery time. Confused she looked around. All she saw was darkness. Where in heaven's name was she?

She turned her head slightly. She was a dark room that smelt a bit fishy and her hands were tied in front of her.

Amanda began to panic; her last memory was being on Enya. *Where the hell am I?* She scrambled around, trying to find a way out in the darkness of the room. Suddenly a door opened and light flooded in.

"Ahh, I see my little guest has finally woken up from her little accident on the horse," said a dry female voice.

"Who is that?" Amanda shouted out, holding her hand up to the light to shield it from her eyes."

"Oh dear, don't tell me that you don't remember me. Well you are not about to forget me again."

"N-Natasha?" stammered Amanda. "What am I doing here? This isn't funny."

"Really? Grant's chubby little fiancée trussed up like a pig. I would say it's hilarious."

"You bitch! What's the big idea? Kidnapping people is a crime! What kind of sick, twisted game is this? " Amanda was starting to suspect this was more than a prank.

"It's a not a game, more a minor business involving you

disappearing forever."

"What? Are you crazy? You won't get away with this!"

Natasha smiled maliciously, "But darling, I already have."

Natasha looked at Amanda, her smirk widening, "Grant has more enemies than you may think darling. All it took was a few phones calls to the right people, and here you are."

With one last disdainful look in her direction Natasha turned and walked away, but before she could close the door Amanda asked, "Why? Why would you do this?"

"Grant Hamilton is one arrogant man," Natasha said. "He actually thought he could replace me with your overweight self and make me the laughing stock of society without consequence.

"By shipping you off, not only will he have to deal with heartbreak, but he'll have to deal with never knowing what happened to you, it will drive him insane."

"This doesn't make any sense; he isn't in love with me."

"Oh but he is," replied Natasha.

"No," Amanda said, shaking her head, but the rest of her reply came out as a whisper.

"I overhear him on the phone with one of his brothers. He was gushing over how he orchestrated a mail-order bride scheme just so he could meet you. Eager like a puppy about your pending nuptial. It was disgusting."

The news shocked Amanda to her core. "But..." she tried to say something, but she could not get anything else to leave her mouth. Something finally clicked within Amanda's head, the fog lifting from her mind all in a matter of a few seconds. If Grant had known from the very beginning...if he had planned this...then maybe...he felt something for her. *I've got to get out of here!*

Natasha began to shut the door again, but then she paused like she remembered something.

"I almost forgot," she said as she motioned to someone standing out in the hall. Within a few moments a man holding a syringe came into the dark room and walked towards Amanda.

"A little present to help you sleep. Next time you wake up, you'll be thousands of miles away and likely some fat man's whore."

The guy holding the syringe came at Amanda, and she started to struggle. One swift kick to the man's shins and he was cussing. He lunged at her again, grabbed her roughly and banged her against the back wall. Pain shot through her head. Amanda slumped to the ground and blacked out.

EPILOGUE

G rant had been busy all day organizing a surprise for Amanda. He knew she must be overwhelmed by the events that had unfolded. If he couldn't tell her how much he loved her with words yet, he intended to show her. He knew this was happening too fast for her, but the thought of possibly losing Amanda made him determined to ensure they were married by the end of the week.

Grant knew something was wrong the minute his limousine reached the manor. Manny Wright, his estate manager, was usually a very calm and efficient person. He was standing outside the front doors, fidgeting with something in his hands.

"What is wrong?" Grant asked hurriedly.

"It's Miss Cardwell," replied Manny.

"What about her?" asked Grant, his voice rising.

"She went out riding one of the horses," Manny replied, still fidgeting with his hands. "But an hour later the horse made its way back to the stables without Miss Cardwell."

"Well, have you searched the grounds?" Grant's voice was laced with worry.

"Yes we have sir. We've searched them twice over; Miss Cardwell is nowhere to be found. But we found this." Manny handed him a bloody paper.

Dear Grant.
Sorry about the short notice. Took Amanda for a stroll, don't expect her back in this lifetime. I hope her disappearance haunts you.
Toodaloo.

Grant felt anger burning through his veins. Someone had hurt Amanda. Her blood was still wet on the paper. *Someone had hurt Amanda.* Grant leaned his head into his hands, his eyes closed. *Someone had HURT Amanda.*

***

"CHASE, YOU HAVE TO HELP ME!"

Grant knew if there was someone who could help him crack this mystery it was his brother Chase Hamilton. Chase was the CEO of a multimillion dollar security company.

"You need to calm down and think logically Grant. Who would leave this kind of message? The way it is worded is personal, almost like the kidnapper wants you to know it's them. The wording contains a lot of rage. Think."

"Rage...the only one I can think of is...Natasha." The name came to Grant's mind unbidden. He remembered their last encounter, and how jealous she had been of Amanda.

"I have to go, thanks little brother."

Grant hung up and re-dialed Natasha's number.

"Well, hello Grant," said Natasha.

"Don't play games with me Natasha," Grant fumed, "what have you done with Amanda?"

"Why would you accuse me of doing anything to your precious Amanda?" Natasha asked her voice laced with mock surprise.

"Natasha," Grant said, trying desperately to appear humble, "please, just let me know what you've done with her. We can work this out."

"No, no we can't Grant," replied Natasha, all pretense of surprise disappeared from her voice to be replaced with cold anger. "We can't work things out. However I'll let you know where you can tell her goodbye from, but there's no saving her."

"Fine," said Grant, "just tell me where I can say goodbye."

"You'll find her at the Jacksonville Port, shipping out for sea on a ship. Have fun trying to find her. Toodaloo Grant."

"Damn you Natasha, I swear next time I see you again I'll—" The phone went dead.

Still fuming that Natasha would dare harm what was his, Grant ran for his Ferrari and sped towards the harbor. If he could get there in time he may just be able to get to Amanda.

It took another hour to get something out of the harbor master. In the end he confirmed that there was only one ship outbound for the next 5 hours, it was departing from quay 52. Grant started sprinting towards the quay. As he got closer he saw a freight ship making preparations to set sail. He started racing towards it, but before he could make it to the ship, a horn sounded and the cargo freighter began to pull away from the harbor. "No!" yelled Grant, as he kept sprinting, "Stop!"

***

AMANDA WOKE UP in a brightly lit room that looked like it was taken straight out of a thousand and one nights. She stumbled out of the bed she had woken up in and made her way over to the window. The heat was unbearable, and it didn't help clear up her cloudy mind.

Looking out of the window, her mouth dropped open. For miles in all directions the only thing Amanda could see was sand.

MONTANA NIGHT

PART 2

CHAPTER 1

Amanda Cardwell woke up in a brightly lit room that looked taken straight out of *Arabian Nights*. A lock of auburn hair tumbled across her face; she hurriedly hooked it behind her throbbing ear with shaky hands. She stumbled out of the four-poster bed and made her way over to a big bay window to the opposite side of the room. Looking out of the window, her mouth dropped open. *Oh my gosh!*

For miles in all directions the only thing Amanda could see was sand.

She started racking her foggy brain for an explanation. *How did I get here?* Her brain stubbornly refused to give her an answer. *Think Amanda!*

Dread started spreading its clammy tenterhooks through her veins. However hard she tried her brain was not about to co-operate. She couldn't remember a thing. *Calm down.*

Taking a couple of deep breaths she realized it wasn't true. She did remember some things. She knew that adding two and two would get you four, that the sun always rose in the east, and that the Chicago Cubs were never going to win the World Series again. And she knew her own name. Well, the first one at least. She had no idea what her last name was, how she'd ended up in this room, or why she could smell rosemary and myrrh incense so thickly in the air.

Scared with all that wasn't rushing back to her, Amanda surged to her feet. Frantically she looked around. She spotted a beautiful ornate door and decided it was better to find somewhere to hide quickly and *then* try to figure out what had happened to her. As she tiptoed through the door she stopped right in her track. A sliver of panic ran down her spine.

Her surroundings looked like she'd fallen onto the set of *Arabian Nights*. The women staring back at her---and there had to be almost four dozen---were gorgeous. Thin but with heaving bosoms, skin bronzed from the sun and from their natural complexion, and the flattest midriffs she'd ever seen. Amanda noted that she was dressed in a long black flowing robe, like she remembered seeing in a lot of Middle Eastern women, minus the head coverings. Meanwhile, everyone else was decked out in flowing pants that made her think of genies.

With almost fifty exotic beauties surrounding her, bedecked in bangles and the finest silks, she felt like the odd duckling. Tentatively she ran her hands down her body. Relieved, she noted that she had been blessed with an hourglass shaped figure. But it was clear that she was *oh so* far from supermodel size. *Can't complain about the boobs or the junk in the trunk though.*

Arching her neck around, she groaned again at the way her pants fit too snugly. Something else flicked through her memory and Amanda threw off the black garment covering her.

Underneath, she still wore plain jeans and a white T-shirt. *Clearly I am not part of this harem. So what am I doing here?*

A few of the women were edging towards her and Amanda stumbled backwards. She turned around and ran over the collection of thick red and gold rugs, woven with the most intricate of patterns, and desperately looked for another way out of the immense room. The windows were covered in thick bars made of iron, at the sight her heart almost stopped. Wherever she was, she wasn't leaving any time soon, maybe not ever again. *Perfect.*

She didn't know who she was, and she didn't know where she was except a desert. Tears welled up in her eyes and she slid down the wall and to the floor.

The sea of inhumanly gorgeous women parted from in front of her. An elderly matron, rotund and shapeless under her coverings, knelt down before her. On either side of the woman stood guards. Their necks were the size of tree trunks, and they carried both scimitars on their left hips and nine mils in a holster over their right shoulders.

Nope. She was never leaving. *I've really done it this time.*

That was the last thought to cross her mind before darkness overtook her. But reality came quickly crashing back through smelling salts from hell. The stench could only be described as ten times worse than sewers. *Right, clearly fainting isn't the answer. I'm still here.*

As hard as she was trying to go back to blissful unconsciousness the women surrounding her didn't seem to want to let her. The army of beauties was babbling away in Arabic. So they were making zero sense to Amanda. The only discernible words were *Mr. Assad* and *doctor.* As the guards motioned with their scimitars towards the door, Amanda assumed they wanted to take her to some kind of examination. By now, her head was throbbing, and she was fervently hoping this examination was going to be external only.

***

DR. ASSAD TURNED OUT to be a kindly little man with lines at the corner of his eyes and a long graying beard that tickled Amanda's arms as he leaned in to take her temperature.

"Ms. Cardwell, how are you feeling today?" Dr. Assad prodded as he listened to her chest. Idly, Amanda wondered if he could feel it race as badly as she did.

"Wretched. Confused. I can't remember who I am. I…well. I don't know what to think. How did I get here?" A terrifying thought, straight from the cheesiest movies she had ever seen, flashed through her mind. "Am I here to be some dirty old sheikh's whore?" Amanda blurted, blushed, and then clamped her mouth shut. *Please, please tell me I'm wrong.*

The doctor smiled back at her, making his eyes twinkle just a bit, almost like Santa. "I am just an old man, Ms. Cardwell, but I understand. I think you've gotten quite the wrong impression of Master Alid."

"Master Alid?"

"Yes, Sheikh Samir Ben Alid, he is the Master of this harem. I've known Samir since he was a child. I was first his father's personal physician."

"Oh, I'm sorry."

Dr. Assad smiled indulgently as he pulled out a pen light to inspect her eyes; she blinked at the onslaught. "His father is very much alive as are his three brothers. He is a young man by my standards. When he moved to Oman, I chose to go with him. He's a good man, works hard to make sure his family's company gives to worthy charities, and the way he is with Jasmine--"

It suddenly felt cold in the room. "Is she also in the harem?"

"His little sister, but you'll meet more people here soon enough," he finished, going over to his counter. "Ms. Cardwell, you don't appear to have anything wrong with you apart from your concussion."

She rubbed her head as if a knot would magically appear there. "I don't doubt I had a concussion. This amnesia must have come from somewhere. I can't recall family or friends. My life before waking up here is shrouded in darkness. It is like someone has erased part of my past. "

"A serious blow to the head like you had can lead to retrograde amnesia. Retrograde amnesia means you have lost memories for events PRIOR to the head injury accident. For some people, the amnesia can cover just a minute or even a few seconds. For other people, like in your case, amnesia may affect longer periods of time.

"What does this mean? Am I ever going to get my memory back?"

"As people get better from their head injuries, long-term memories tend to return. If you are lucky, your memory will be triggered by smell, sound, or something visual and you will be yourself again."

"And if I am unlucky?"

"Then your memories will return like fragments of a jigsaw puzzle; bits and pieces returning in random order."

Amanda sat in silence for several minutes as the doctor continued his examination. Every nerve ending of her body was screaming at her to run. Taking a deep breath, she willed her heart to stop thudding in her chest. What she needed now were facts. "How did I get here if I wasn't taken?"

"Of course, in the Middle East we are all in the business of stealing Western women," the doctor replied harshly, the insult clear in his voice.

Amanda blushed and looked away, realizing how terrible her accusations sounded when said aloud. "I apologize. I didn't mean it that way, to play on stereotypes. Still, I wake up behind bars literally so what am I supposed to think?"

"Your family accrued substantial gambling debts as I've heard it. Master Alid paid them and sent your father to gambling rehabilitation. You agreed to come live as part of the harem for two years as part of the compensation. He offered other methods, but you were quite insistent."

"I was?" Amanda exclaimed, her brow creased in confusion.

"Assuredly from what I heard. He saved your family and you wanted to come be a part of his life here from gratitude. Whatever you might think...Master Alid is a great man."

Amanda sighed and was grateful when Dr. Assad left to allow her some time to reconcile with what she had just been told. One single thought lingered in her mind.

She did this to herself.

CHAPTER 2

The hot summer sun blazed down on Billionaire Tycoon Grant Hamilton as he got out of the Learjet in Tel Aviv. He wasn't that fond of the Middle East. While there were certain elements of the culture, and especially in his younger years, the women that he enjoyed, the constant sun and heat wore at him. It wasn't like Florida either, where the heat was interspersed with rain, clouds, or pleasant breezes that came off the ocean at night. Here in the Middle East, it was sandblasting furnace hot, almost constantly.

"*Barukh ha-ba* Mr. Hamilton. I trust your flight was comfortable?" an older Israeli man greeted him. His name was Levi, with no last name. He was a retired Mossad agent who now worked in the private sector. Both Grant's younger brothers Alexander and Chase had endorsed his skills.

After pouring over the records of the Harbormaster in Florida, Grant had called on Chase, who used his private contacts to trace the ship to the Middle East. From there though, Chase was lost, as his security company CorpSec focused mainly in the Americas and East Asia. Alexander had offered to step in and help, but he was currently handling an assignment for the CIA. It left Grant by himself, although both brothers swore to drop everything and come if needed. Their last piece of assistance was Levi's name and contact information.

"*Shalom* Master Levi, I appreciate your hospitality. The journey was as tolerable as possible under the circumstances. As this is a matter of urgency let's move straight to business. What have your sources discovered?"

"We have traced her to Oman, but more than that I cannot say for sure. We know the specific men who took your fiancée, but so far we have not been able to track down their whereabouts. Do you have any idea who might have wanted to kidnap your fiancée beyond this Natasha that your staff mentioned?"

"No," Grant replied in a terse voice. "My business dealings have been world-wide, and not all of those deals have ended with all parties happy. However I can't imagine any of my competitors or ex-business partners doing anything like this." He could not disguise the strained tone of his voice.

"I have experience in such matters, Mr. Hamilton," Levi continued, leading him towards a small building off to the side of the main terminal. "My associates are doing their best to find the exact location of the girl's kidnappers as we speak."

"Amanda," Grant hissed, his anger surprising them both. "She's not 'the girl,' she's not just my fiancée. She is a person and her name is Amanda."

Levi nodded, sympathy clouding his features. "Of course. Amanda. If I may give some professional advice?"

Grant took a deep breath. He knew he was being unreasonable and difficult with people who didn't have to help him. But guilt gnawed his innards like a rabid dog. *I should have protected her.*

Not answering until Levi had pulled open the door and led him inside, he sighed in appreciation of the air conditioning. "Go ahead, Levi. Please accept my apologies for becoming so heated."

"Apology accepted. Emotions are not a bad thing, Mr. Hamilton. My people have learned that without the passions of your heart, your enemies will eventually win. But, you cannot let your passion's flame so fiercely as to consume you both. Then you will definitely lose."

Grant nodded, his resolve reconfirmed. "Wise words, Levi. No wonder my brothers like you."

"Mr. Chase only has an affinity for me because he and my son share similar bad tastes in music," Levi said with a smile, leading Grant towards his company's operations center. Inside, Grant saw three other people, two stunningly beautiful Israeli women and a man who Grant thought may have been an Arab of some sort.

Levi made introductions. "Mr. Hamilton, let me introduce my intelligence staff. The two ladies you see are Talia and Roni Ben-David, twin sisters. They are computer hackers whose skill is only surpassed by their matchless beauty. The handsome gentleman with them Rashn, who like me prefers to go by only one name."

"Thank you all for your assistance," Grant replied, the cultured tones and niceties of society falling into place with unconscious ease. He may not have liked the Middle East for the weather, but he hadn't completed all the deals he had without at least some manners. "You have my gratitude."

"Levi, Talia was able to crack into the accounts you asked about," the woman Grant assumed was Roni said immediately.

"We were able to track two separate emails, one to a bar in Abu Dhabi, another to a so far anonymous account in Oman itself. We have names on the kidnappers you requested."

"Do you have their current whereabouts?" Levi asked, a sanguine smile spreading over his face. *Soto voce*, he whispered to Grant. "See? I told you they were good."

"Yes," Talia replied, taking over for her sister. "The sender of the email is on his way to Riyadh at this time."

Grant nodded, and looked over at Rashn. "Do you have any additional information to report?"

The man shook his head, crossing his arms over his chest.

"All right then. Levi, my jet can be refueled and ready to fly in an hour. It looks like we're heading to Riyadh." *I'm coming for you, just hold one. Be safe.*

Levi nodded, a grin breaking out wider on his face. "It's been a while. I wonder if the Saudis still remember me?"

CHAPTER 3

As Amanda was walked back to the main harem compound, she found herself surrounded again. Out of the sea of concubines an older woman stepped forward, reached out, and stroked her hair. Amanda took a step backwards.

"Who are you people?" she demanded, hating how her voice wouldn't come out as more than a whimper. "Do you live in this harem?"

A woman sashayed out from behind the taller of the two guards. Her hips swayed with seductive authority; she oozed sensuality and knew it. Hazel eyes heavy with mascara bore into her own eyes and Amanda gulped. Why did she find her even scarier than the guards with weapons? She stopped, looking as if she had swallowed something exceedingly bitter.

"I am Nadia, supreme mistress of this estate. Our master, the honorable Sheikh Samir Ben-Alid, has ordered us to welcome you to his harem." Having taken a moment to regain her composure, she straightened up swaying her hips, the bangles adorning their slim dimensions jangling for all to hear.

"I find you lacking, American, but the master wishes as he wishes, and his wish is our command."

"Really?" Amanda remarked; pleased at how nonchalant she sounded. She wasn't skinny with fitness model abdominals like Nadia was, but she wasn't going to put up with anyone's stinky attitude either. Whoever she had been, Amanda already knew she was a fighter. She was determined not to reveal to these people exactly how scared she was. Taking a deep breath she added with a smile of defiance, "I don't particularly want to meet him. Maybe another day."

"Foolish girl. It is an honor." Nadia said with disdain. "What you wish stopped mattering the moment you agreed to be here," she continued more calmly, her voice containing an underlying hint of ice.

"So I've been told. I still don't believe I am the kind of person who would want to be locked up in a harem. Seriously, why would I?"

"Because you are a *sharmuta*, a whore who needed rescuing," Nadia snapped. She eyed the older woman standing at her right, her voice calming as she issued her commands. "The bath oils first.... and then find this *bin'nt himaar* something that might hope to fit her."

The older woman nodded, but struggled to bend down to pull off Amanda's T-shirt. Nadia's next command—whatever it was ---was in Arabic, but it was motivating enough for the older woman and several of the other girls to strip Amanda to her underwear. They didn't stop there however, as two of the younger girls started to pull down her panties, while another two held her arms and the third unclasped her bra. Her heavy breasts spilled out like cream topped with a cherry, bouncing delicately at their sudden freedom. Amanda had never felt so humiliated and helpless in her life. An unwelcome blush crept into her cheeks.

Despite the situation, it was Nadia's hot stare, trailing leisurely from her round breasts to the auburn patch between her legs, that made her most uncomfortable.

"Our master likes a shaven *koos*, so your lovely bush will unfortunately have to go." Nadia walked up to her and started caressing her neck leisurely. Amanda thought she was going to melt from the embarrassment. The entire harem was watching in silence. What kind of crazy rabbit hole had she fallen into?

"I…" she stammered her flush deepening to crimson. "Stop it!"

Spying her discomfort, Nadia replied icily. "Master Alid will soon grow tired of you, but no need to worry."

Nadia grinned, but Amanda had seen sharks with friendlier expressions on the Discovery Channel. "When you're found wanting, *sharmuta*, I will get to give you my special brand of attention."

From the look in her eyes, Amanda knew it wasn't punishment Nadia was aiming for. *I need to get the heck out of here.*

***

AFTER WHAT SEEMED like an eternity Amanda found herself oiled, powdered, and getting a manicure from an older woman in the harem. Behind her, two girls took turns with her hair. After shampooing it, they rubbed luxurious conditioners in, rinsing it multiple times before applying scented oils. They tried braiding it in a pair of ropes down her back, but the older of the two girls, whose jet black hair glistened in the steamy heat of the bath and hung straight down the middle of her back, with a beautiful tiger's eye amulet at her copper colored throat, had hated it. After an exchange of heated, foreign words, the younger girl with hair more magenta than red, had pulled everything down. Now they were back to the drawing board. This time, they used curling irons to help pile Amanda's long locks up in an up-do with tendrils raining from it. The older woman had found flower petals and jeweled hair combs to accent everything. She had no living memory of ever looking this beautiful. While she wanted to go home, wherever that was, somehow she couldn't stop herself from wanting to be as beautiful as the women around her were. *No longer the ugly duckling?* she thought, as they showed her the results in a hand mirror. The style was flattering and would please this Master Alid, according to the old woman. Even Amanda could only agree. Odd that she should be concerned by what a mystery sheikh thought of her.

Even though her worst fears had ebbed after her third hour of pampering, she was very aware a man now had the right to do whatever he wanted with her body. *Take a deep breath. You can get through this.*

The tranquil location of the harem, with richly adorned facilities, soft silken clothing, and gilded accents was oddly soothing. So far, it seemed as long as she didn't stare too hard at the guards by the door, Amanda could almost forget she was now property. After Nadia's threats, she had expected to be flogged and set out in some palace square in stocks. Shouldn't Alid that pervert sultan or whatever he was, have burst in here by now to have his way with her? Amanda gulped. *Reality check – Yep. I am still freaked out.*

Nervously, she looked back to the poor magenta-haired girl and was quickly urged to set her head back into place. "I'm sorry. I just…not that I want Nadia to come back, but I thought this would be worse. Was I wrong?"

The oldest woman chuckled. "Nadia speaks angrily, but she was his favorite before. She would dance and Master Alid would fall down at her feet. For years she had been his favorite, but since your arrival, she has found herself in an unfamiliar position."

"It seems," the raven haired woman added, "That this change has caused her personality to come through in new ways, though. Nadia was always a terror. She has very unique tastes and…never mind. Let's just say that I'm glad someone got bumped off the pedestal. She's a – what do you Americans call it – a bitch?"

Amanda burst out laughing "Yes, I guess a bitch is exactly what she is." Both women started laughing uncontrollably. The girl leaned over and bowed her head a bit toward Amanda. "I'm Dyana, by the way. I've been here for a long time, maybe five years. It's not as bad as you think. We've all come of our own free will, often as favors for our families. We're cared for and Master Alid…." Dyana's voice trailed off, as a blush rose to her cheeks.

The magenta-hair girl laughed loudly even as she added the first pins for Amanda's emerald green veil. "What my sister means is that man knows how to pleasure a woman. The worst day isn't joining the harem. It's always when he finds another one. We're still given some access, the lucky ones at least, but once you have a lover of that skill… well being trapped here isn't so bad. We're all spoiled for other men."

"Odella!" Dyana chided. "That's too much. She means that Master is very kind and, ahem, generous."

"Yes, generous enough that I'm stuck here with prison bars and armed guards. You all sound like educated, modern women. Why are you voluntarily staying here as a slave?" Amanda asked, puzzled.

"There are many reasons the women of the Sheikh stay, and many reasons why the Master has guards," the older woman said, working with surprising speed with the pale pink nail polish on Amanda's pinkie. "First, there are many who would seek to steal these girls, to keep them for their own. The guards are far more for their well-being than to keep them from fleeing."

"That all sounds very charming, if you were raised in the Middle East. I still want to go home!"

Odella tutted and finished settling the veil over Amanda's head. It fell to cover her face so that now she could only see through the eye slit. The sheer fabric was very breathable however, and she didn't feel at all stifled by the airy garment. "You don't even know where that is and, believe me Miss; you can't imagine how fortunate you are."

Amanda sighed and wasn't sure what to think. Samir had saved her family. It could be a lie, but then both Dyana and Odella said that Samir was about as amazing as it gets. Hell, Nadia wouldn't be such a jealous bitch if he wasn't worth holding onto.

Speak of the Devil, and she shall appear. Nadia sashayed into the room, heading straight for Amanda. Using just her eyes and a sharp gesture, she commanded the guards, who moved to either side of Amanda, seizing her in their immensely powerful hands.

"Time for your treatment," Nadia said with a seductively, devilish smile.

CHAPTER 4

As she lay tied down to what looked like a X shaped massage table, Amanda felt her heart racing. The humiliation of having all of her clothes stripped off of her for the second time still stung. Tied, Amanda could only stare at the ceiling, glimpsing her crotch as she lay on the table.

Nadia had sent everyone else away, decreeing she would be waxing the *sharmuta* personally before leaving her alone for what seemed like an eternity. Despite straining to release herself, the silk ties Nadia had used held her firmly in place. Exhausted from her futile attempts Amanda stilled. Out of the corner of her eye she could see beautifully ornate shelves and furniture, creams, and lotions. It then dawned on her that whatever this "treatment" was she could not stop what was about to happen. As Amanda wondered what kind of perverted game she was to be exposed to, Nadia walked back into the room. Amanda had never felt so powerless in her life.

Nadia's eyes trailed over her naked body as she walked towards her, causing Amanda to blush. She resolved that whatever was going to happen she would survive and make Nadia pay. With trepidation she clenched her eyes closed and waited for the assault.

Nothing happened.

After what seemed like an eternity she cranked one eye open. Nadia was busily fiddling away with some vials.

"Well are you going to get on with it or what?" Amanda tried to sound defiant, but anxiety spurted through her.

"You are eager for my attention, that is good," replied Nadia. She turned around and unceremoniously started massaging Amanda with a concoction that smelt like evening primrose oil mixed with almond and something else Amanda could not identify.

It felt... marvelous. Amanda almost melted at the pleasure. She hadn't allowed herself to acknowledge how sore and battered she had felt since her awakening. Now Nadia's supple fingers soothed away all the aches, and she almost purred. Confused but determined not to waste time trying to understand the strange goings on she closed her eyes and let herself enjoy the relaxing massage. But soon she noticed something was off. The oil was creating a strange sensation wherever Nadia touched. The sensation grew with every stroke.

"Ah, I see the oil is starting to work its magic," Nadia whispered in her ear. Amanda's eyes popped open.

Nadia was standing *so very close*. Looking her deep in the eyes, she slowly started working the oil around her pubic hair. Making sure she spread her vagina lips to cover every corner. In the process she accidently stroked Amanda's clit. A delicious tendril of desire shot through her body. *How-, what the hell?!*

Confused, Amanda didn't know what to think. She didn't

think she had ever let a woman touch her before. It didn't matter that her memory was gone; she thought she would remember that. Convinced it must have been a mistake, she kept her eyes glued to the harem Mistress.

With deft fingers Nadia continued her ministration by rubbing the liquid concoction over her crotch, spending extra attention on the area around her labia. Nadia's labored breath echoed through the room. With one hand still casually stroking Amanda's crotch, she reached over, smearing some sort of wax from a jar over her entire nether region. Amanda bit her lower lip, confused at what the heck was happening. Embarrassed and convinced she was just misunderstanding; she shut her mouth and closed her eyes. This was a wax and nothing else.

Just as anxiety was giving way to relaxation Nadia accidently pinched her clit trying to spread wax along her vaginal lips. Amanda couldn't help it; the sensations caused her to moan out load, before she could bite it back.

Now wary about what was next to come, Amanda tried to glimpse what Nadia was doing. With concentration the Harem Mistress was spreading the wax mixture evenly so it totally covered all of Amanda's pubic hair. She withdrew her hands momentarily to wipe them clean on a soft terrycloth towel. She then picked up a strip of muslin cloth, and spread it over some of the waxy area on the inside of Amanda's right thigh.

With one swift move Nadia pulled up the cloth, the wax uprooting Amanda's pubic hair, leaving behind a one inch wide strip of smooth, bare skin. Amanda almost bucked off the table. The pain was intense. But what followed, an aftermath of pure desire was what left her gasping. *How is this possible?*

She intuitively knew that she wasn't the type of girl to enjoy casual sex. Despite her denial, she could feel wetness start to seep from her pussy, and the room filled with the scent of her arousal. Nadia accidently stroked her clit again and another tendril of desire shot through her. It was now clear to Amanda, there was nothing accidental about what was happening.

"You are a good little whore. You are almost ready for Master Alid," Nadia said as she dispensed with all pretense. Her fingers started rubbing up and down Amanda's soft labia. She drew her finger up, stroking once over the hooded tenderness of Amanda's clit. The touch wrenching a gasp from Amanda, her eyes flaring open before they settled on Nadia, who continued to chuckle.

"Stop calling me a whore," she groaned, her anger momentarily taking the edge off her desire and allowing her to focus on something besides the fire in her pussy. Nadia just laughed, and smiled devilishly.

The erotic torture continued, as Nadia used almost a dozen strips to take off every bit of hair. By the end, her pubic skin was puffy and swollen, almost as red as the now stripped away pubic hair had been. With the skin baby smooth, Amanda's pussy was painfully sensitive. She could feel the whisper of the air over her skin and her engorged clit.

"Nice and hairless. Now let us make sure your pussy is as sweet as the Master likes it." Nadia purred. She slid her slender index finger unceremoniously inside Amanda's wet tunnel. The penetration was enough to cause Amanda to squirm on the table, her hips rising of their own accord; her movement a silent plea for more penetration.

Nadia laughed. Looking her straight in the eyes, she brought the finger coated in Amanda's juices to her lips and licked it off.

"Not bad. But I think we can get you sweeter still, little slut," she muttered as she moved to get something from the shelf. Amanda felt tears of frustration spring to her eyes. There was no denying it. Her body was humming with desire. She must be some sort of sex-crazed slut. *Why else would I be feeling this way?*

Nadia picked up a small phallus shaped wooden tool. It looked like a honey dipper spoon except the tip had shallower grooves. She dipped it in the oil concoction, and once it was nicely coated she turn towards Amanda again.

Unable to control herself she could feel her pussy weep copious juices at the approach of the Harem Mistress. The exotic tortures gave Amada no respite; her nimble fingers spread her vagina lips and inserted the tool. Amanda gasped at the delicious intrusion.

Unable to control her responses she moaned with abandon as the tool was pumped, then twisted and turned in her pussy. She could feel her stomach muscles tighten, her pussy weeping copious juices. The delicious torture went on for what seemed like an eternity.

But as abruptly as the stimulation had started it stopped. Nadia stood back, an evil smirk on her lips. Her pink tongue whipped out and licked the honey dipper coated with Amanda's juices. "Yes, now you are ready," she whispered. "You taste very good," she stated in a hoarse voice before turning and leaving. The room was almost silent, only the soft sobbing gasps of Amanda's breathing making any noise at all.

***

NADIA CLOSED the treatment room door, leaning hard against it, her breath labored. The images of what she had just done, combined with the taste of Amanda, which still lingered on her tongue, had her panting hard. Unable to resist she closed her eyes and inserted her hand between her legs. The slippery wetness between her thighs made it almost impossible to get a good grip but she finally found her pleasure pearl and rhythmically started pinching it. She nearly sunk to the ground from the strength of her own orgasm.

Gasping she straightened her clothes. It would not do to be found in such a state in the harem halls. As she walked away she was satisfied she had prepared the girl sufficiently for the attention of their Master. Luckily enough Master Alid did not know that the assignment he had tasked her for was one she would undertake with relish.

After all, her secret preference had always been the fairer sex. Whistling she continued sashaying down the hall.

CHAPTER 5

"He'll take a lot of discipline, my sheikh," the trainer said, bowing low.

Sheikh Samir Ben-Alid considered the little man before him. He was of no consequence to him, so few people were. His family was one of the lucky few in Oman who had their hands truly in the oil industry. The nation, unlike their neighbors to the north in Saudi Arabia, had never developed a robust oil exporting business. Luckily for him, his father had possessed a great vision, bringing it to fruition first through the possession and domination of the port at Muscat, and then through carefully nurturing the Alid dynasty's oil empire.

It left him wealthy beyond most people's wildest imaginings, but it also left Samir bored and painfully unfulfilled. When he could purchase anything, what challenge was there to life anymore?

Sighing, he straightened the scarves on his head. To wish for the heat to abate was foolish. It was high summer and the heat would be soaring past one hundred and twenty degrees Fahrenheit today. All the more reason to be away from this dusty arena and back to his compound. At least pleasures for the tongue and of the flesh awaited him there, a way to while away the time and escape the heat.

Samir finally nodded at the horse's trainer. "I'd like a chance to inspect him myself."

"Yes sir, of course," the little man replied, bowing again and slinking toward the other stalls.

Bowing… they were always bowing. He was an Alid, and no one ever forgot their place. Not his underlings, and certainly not his lovers. Carefully, Samir reached out and ran a hand down the neck and shoulder of the Arabian. The stallion neighed and almost reared back, but Samir had been around horses his entire life. He didn't yield to the tantrum. Instead, he grabbed the horse's lead in his powerful hand and held it tightly, even as he stared the animal in its eyes.

Holding up his other hand, he commanded the stallion firmly. Samir did not shout. That would never do, it would just encourage it to bolt. No, this was a promise, a contract. He was master, and would lead and care for the horse if only the steed would honor and obey him. In all aspects of his life, whether it be taking on a servant, breaking a horse, or finding a new woman, it was always the same.

"Tornado, stop. You will quit panicking."

The horse stopped trying to rear and stayed firmly planted on all four feet. It shuffled a bit between its back and front legs, but did not attempt to rear again. Samir smiled and patted its neck with firm, strong strokes, letting his fingers ruffle through its mane. Within moments, the horse was gentle and calm.

"Very good, my steed. You know the correct tone at least. Breaking you, that shall truly be no challenge."

The horse nickered, a whistle of air hissing through its nostrils but did little else. Quickly, Samir made his way around the animal, cautious to give it proper warning and constant communication as he assessed its hocks and back hooves. Strong, well-muscled, and no visible injuries or defects that sycophantic little weasel clearly would have hidden.

"Very good."

The fact that it was the offspring of two champion lines, including a Tevis Cup winning grandfather and a World Equestrian Games champion mother was better still.

By the time Samir made a full circle around his newest acquisition, the insufferable horse trainer and his own assistant were entering back into the stall. "He has fine lines. Both of his parents are of pure Arabian blood, yes?"

"Yes, sir, only the finest of Arabian bloodlines and if you---"

"He'll do," Samir replied, nodding toward Yusef, his most trusted servant, both head of his security team and the only other man in his employ who stood close to his own six feet. "Give Farzod whatever he needs to finish the transaction, and make sure Tornado is delivered to my personal stables by the end of the week. I have a delivery at home to attend to."

As Samir walked back across the stables he mused to himself. It was just all too easy. A mere acquisition no longer presented a challenge to him. From childhood, he need only ask, and his father and mother would lavish him with anything his heart desired. As a child he had all the sweets he could eat, the best toys and games. As a teenager, he'd had a Ferrari by fifteen and an Aston Martin by sixteen. At thirty-five, he'd lost count of his garage and all the treasures therein.

If it wasn't for an internal steel, the desire to prove himself outside the pampered palace of his parents, he would have easily fallen into the decadent, corrupt life he had seen the few boys he could have ever called his peers fall into. Instead, he had devoted himself starting at the age of twelve to physical pursuits and the martial arts, as at least there he saw men who built themselves not through money, but through their own sweat. In wrestling, he found a pursuit in which poor men could become champions, and rich men humbled. He refused to be humbled, and soon his skill was on par with many of the best in the Middle East.

But, like the cars, like the horses, the challenge was gone for him. His life now seemed to be an endless cycle of ennui. It was enough to make him shudder as he pondered the future.

With women it was the same way. His harem currently boasted close to fifty members, and, in turn, he'd indulged in every desire a person could name. He'd had women of almost every nationality, every body shape, every hair or eye color. There was almost nothing left for him. Well, almost. There were some lines he had no interest in. Despite the practices of some of his "social peers," he never took a girl underage, and he never left any of his former bedmates destitute, nor did he physically force himself on them. He had no interest in truly scarring any of his lovers and concubines, not emotionally or physically. Sometimes they skirted lines, but that was the fun of it. Consent was always easy to get. For most of the women, they took one look at the opulence of his houses, his own handsome appearance, and they all practically fell to their knees to worship his cock.

It was what made it all so damned boring. When he had been a wrestler, the finest accomplishments came when he conquered an opponent who refused to just roll over, who fought back and provided him with a true battle. He wished for the same in a woman, a lover who wouldn't just spread her legs like a common whore at the sight of his body and his bank account. The challenge, the sweetest of victories, lay in a successful seduction.

He hoped he could have a challenge now.

***

BACK AT THE MAIN FLOOR of his estate, Samir oversaw a very special and particular delivery. The mattress was the best in the world, flown in yesterday as a special delivery from the maker in California. It was double quilted and could only be fitted with the deepest pocketed sheets. He already had the fine silk sheets set aside for it. He wanted it to complement his next bedmate. He'd only caught a glimpse of Amanda Cardwell this morning, a buxom redhead with an amazing ass he was already fantasizing about. It had taken an impossible amount of self-discipline to allow his number one concubine, Nadia, to move her into the harem quarters, and have her prepared in the beads and veils befitting a lover such as she would become.

When his men had brought her in, still unconscious, her body sprawled across the Persian rug with her hair framing her creamy complexion like a fiery halo, his first instinct was to turn her over and plow her like a brood mare, plundering her body until he spilled his seed into her. *That wouldn't give you the satisfaction of the seduction, nor of the victory over Hamilton.* The thought had helped stave off his lust, but just barely.

Watching Nadia barked orders to the assembled movers, clad in her colorful *dishdasha* that set her apart from so many of the common women clad in their plain black *abaya*, he knew that his plan would be successful. He would christen his bed and, with that, claim Amanda Cardwell as his own, until she never remembered the accursed Grant Hamilton again.

The culmination of today's events had started years ago, as the two young billionaires were still the young scions of their respective families. Traveling through similar social circles, their rivalry had been organic, both men having the combination of respect and personal pride that ensured a consistent game of one-upmanship regardless of the competition. Samir thought the matter had been settled when Grant had started dating his little sister Amirah, with high hopes of a marriage. The rival billionaire had broken his sister's heart, she now lived secluded with Samir's parents, her honor and that of the family forever besmirched. *And her virtue!* Samir's lips thinned with anger. *Vengeance is mine old boy.* Amanda Cardwell was now in his clutches and he had no intention of returning her intact.

He felt a slight twinge at forcing his people to play in the charade he had set up. Even his trusted Yusef and Nadia did not know the true depths of his plans.

The thought of his revenge and pending conquest quieted down the twinges his conscience sometimes gave him. Dr. Assad had informed him of Amanda's condition. It could not be clearer that this was destined to happen *Insha'Allah* (God willing*)*.

Yes, he wasn't only going to possess Hamilton's woman in every physical way possible; he was going to ensure that by the time she got her memories back she didn't want to leave. *The ultimate victory.*

He chuckled, as a thought crossed his mind. The Western cultures always said that revenge was a dish best served cold, but

Samir knew better. It was best when scorching hot, and in the desert, it was very hot indeed.

CHAPTER 6

Samir looked on in anticipation as Nadia marched in with Amanda following behind her. Usually, Nadia made the blood flow fast and freely to his cock, with her sensual manner that spoke of her voracious sexual appetites, but now, even in the tight turquoise top and low slung silken dancing pants she wore, she did nothing for him. The American redhead? Now she was another matter. Amanda didn't walk with the same seductive sway that Nadia had, she walked like an American, very no-nonsense, focused only on getting from one location to another. Still, the violet silk of her harem robes clung to her in all the right ways. His cock swelled in his pants as he looked her over, and he turned away before either woman could notice his lack of control.

But it was Amanda's sharp green eyes staring back at him from behind her veil that intrigued him the most. Her eyes were so complex, simultaneously full of fear and disgust, but also…there was something there, a heat in the way she appraised him that had nothing to do with him being her nominal captor. Nadia had done well. His little fire cracker was still in the aftermath of arousal.

After patiently waiting and planning ever since Amirah's shame had been revealed, and his competitive rivalry had crystallized into hatred, he would finally exact his revenge.

"Nadia, take the guards and go," he ordered as soon as Amanda sat down to his right.

"Master Alid, I can always stay. This one has such a defiant mouth already."

"That's good," he replied, picking up Amanda's right hand and bringing it to his lips to kiss. She stilled beneath him, but allowed it, all the time her eyes trained on the scimitars his guard carried.

Samir knew the swords were a bit of grandiosity, but he loved affectation and his heritage. Besides, it definitely made the correct statement to people who considered crossing him.

"But Master—"

He narrowed his eyes at his head concubine. Nadia had been his favored pet for years, her enthusiasm for unusual carnal delights beyond satisfying, and her imagination matched only by his own. Still, she was forgetting her place. "I said leave us."

She bowed her head. "As you will, Master," she said, her hurt feelings scantly hidden. She and the guards hurried out of the dining room, leaving him and Amanda to themselves. Samir noted to himself that he would have to have a private discussion with Nadia later, to assure her she was still in his favor. She was not just a longtime lover, she was a trusted assistant, and regardless of the situation with Amanda Cardwell, he couldn't lose Nadia. Dismissing the issue from his mind, he turned to his conquest.

"Soon, I'll have my chef bring out some filet mignon. I thought something from your homeland might make some of this transition easier."

"Who are you?" she asked, chin defiantly held high.

"You do not remember me?" The thought of how easy her amnesia made his plan, had Samir smiling internally with satisfaction.

"I can't remember anything from the last six months and only bits and piece of anything prior to that. Your Dr. Ahmed says I have retrograde amnesia."

"Well, that is unfortunate. Nevertheless, that does not negate our agreement. I am Sheihk Samir Ben Alid and you are Amanda Granger. Your father's debts cleared and you as part of my harem for two years."

"I don't even remember my father. For all I know he is a first grade asshole and he sold me to this bondage."

"Or maybe you love him very much and will regret seeing him thrown into prison once you get your memory back? *Habibi*, let's not fight. Maybe you just need a reminder of how I make you feel?" Samir liked the chase, but a chase without reward was just frustration. He lived for a good hard fuck in a pussy as exquisite as hers had to be. While he was a patient man, patience was only a virtue for so long. He stood, even as his help entered and placed the steak and rice dishes on an oaken side table. Coming around to Amanda's side, he leaned down, and with his fingers unfastened the jeweled veil, wanting to see his future lover without the masking effects of the silk. His first thought was he needed to thank Dyana and Odella, their work was excellent. While they had started with a truly marvelous beauty before, the two girls had taken marvelous and elevated it to divine.

Her hair, a fiery auburn that matched his desires, was swept up into a bun with softly curled tendrils raining from it. Her coloring was set off by silver combs adorned with emeralds and white rose petals in her hair. She was a peerless beauty, a figure from a fairy tale, a goddess.

Leaning in further, Samir kissed the pulse point just below her right earlobe. "You, Amanda, are perfect. Has anyone ever told you that?"

***

Amanda almost panicked at his words. She felt herself shrink from the sheer magnetism of his watchful smile. After the "treatment" administered by Nadia she had come prepared for anything. However, from the moment she had laid eyes on Samir, she had known any number of women would willingly have thrown themselves at his feet for the opportunity to spend one night with him. He looked devilishly handsome, broad shoulders filling the expanse of his garb seductively. When her eyes had met his, she had frozen. He had unusual gray eyes, but what took her breath away was the desire blazing through them. Her clit was still shamefully sensitive from her recent orgasm; it wouldn't take a lot for him to convince her to surrender to him. She knew she was in big trouble. *Oh, stop staring at him before you make him want to rape you.*

The logical part of her mind concluded that he wouldn't have laid out this romantic feast if his intention was to take what he wanted. Clearly somehow he wanted the illusion of consent. Chiding herself that she even for a moment forgot this was *so not* a social event she set her chin in a stubborn line.

"I am no man's whore." Somehow it felt like she had said those words before, to another man, in another time. She glared up at him, her gaze challenging.

"*Habibi*, no sane man would ever mistake you for a whore," Samir whispered, one hand delicately caressing her breast through the thin fabric of her tunic. The breath left her lungs in one long rush as delicious tendrils of heat followed the path of his fingers.

Amanda bit her lower lip in an effort to stop herself from groaning. Her nipple pebbled under the wisp of silk.

"No… I," she started, but it was all she was able to get out. He nibbled on her ear lobe and pinched her right nipple oh-so-carefully, the pain and pleasure mingling deliciously making Amanda's breath quicken. Her arms drifted up, pulling him into her, unable to resist the inferno he was creating in her loins. *Oh my gosh.* Her body, already primed by Nadia, craved Samir's touch. *I need to remember.* She needed to remember. Remember what? Then it hit her. *We are in the Middle East. I'm in a harem. If I give myself this easily to this man, he is going to treat me like some unpaid whore for the rest of my stay.*

"Please, stop," she whimpered, as she leaned back from him, her neck exposed as his playground. Her pulse was beating erratically as he nipped and nibbled on her neck.

***

DESPITE HER VOCAL resistance to what Samir knew would be his inevitable victory, Amanda moaned, like a contented kitten. Samir knew he was going to need to sample Amanda soon or explode from need. He kept sucking at her neck, hoping to leave a mark, perhaps several. She was his now and everyone needed to know it. Her moans echoed across the room, and her nipples were engorged and rigid in his grasp. He lifted her easily from her chair, setting her on the table as he sought more, wanting to see her entire body under his gaze, open to him. Samir's desire flared, the sound of his newest conquest so close to completion.

Samir grew too greedy, moving too quickly as his desire flared high, costing him his self-control. He slipped his right hand down to the waistband of her pants, ignoring the way her hands clenched at his approach. Amanda stiffened again, but her moans increased in pitch the more he played with her areola underneath the silk with his left hand. "No...wait," Amanda begged placing her hands on his wrists.

"No, I think you're more than ready." Samir replied, forcing his hand underneath the waistband of her pants to find the smooth hairless expanse of her silken pussy lips.

She startled at his touch and pushed back, her feet coming up to push away at his legs. She was too shocked to keep her balance, instead becoming entangled in the tablecloth and tumbling to the floor, with a bang. Although clearly dazed, she frantically started crawling away on trembling hands.

The sight of her desperate attempt of flight was like cold water poured over Samir's flaming lust. Shame engulfed him. He was known for being an extremely patient and experienced lover, but somehow his renowned self-control in bed had flown out the window. Amanda Cardwell was proving to be more intoxicating than wine.

He knelt cautiously next to her, and pushed the stunning auburn locks back from her heart shaped face. Amanda's entrancing green eyes burned with fury back at him. "Amanda, forgive me."

"I said 'wait.' What was so hard about that, you arrogant aristocrat?"

"I thought---"

"Get away from me," she shouted, standing unsteadily. She weaved in front of him, almost falling, and he reached out, taking her in his arms to steady her. She fought for a moment, before collapsing against him.

"Then what did you mean to happen?" she hissed. There were tears swimming in her eyes, tangling on her long lashes, each one sending daggers into Samir's heart.

"I'm sorry, *habibi*. I should have exercised better control." He truly meant it. He abhorred men who were capable of harming women. Women were delicate creatures, made to be cherished and lavished.

"I just met you. My body might yearn for you, but I don't remember you. I won't let you possess my body before you possess my heart, never mind what I agreed to," Amanda stammered as fear started releasing its grip on her.

Samir was stunned. He hadn't meant to make her uncomfortable, not like that. He had never met a woman who had resisted him or wanted to resist him. *Such fire.* As his gazed trailed over her creamy skin and flaming hair he felt his cock hardening, even after what had just transpired. Embarrassed he shifted legs. *She was like flowing lava and a tornado combined.*

Yusef brought in the doctor, and Samir stood to leave, giving the doctor and Amanda privacy. "I meant to give you more pleasure than imagined. Forgive me."

"No." Amanda turned her gaze away, and the doctor implored Samir with his eyes to leave, lest her emotions cause her further harm.

In the hallway, Samir's mind replayed the whole disastrous evening. Never in his entire life, starting at the age of thirteen, had a woman said 'No' as more than a token resistance in a sexual game, and never had a woman looked upon him with such fury. He was ashamed to realize he now wanted this woman more than ever. *Maybe even by any means necessary.*

Even as he denied the thoughts stirred by his mind, another part of him, the darker side that he rarely listened to, whispered something else though. He had seen, even as she was cursing him and gazing at him in fury, her hands drifting towards the marks on her throat and jaw line, where he had kissed her with so much passion. She caressed the marks, and the dark beast inside him knew she had enjoyed his touch, and it hungered for more.

CHAPTER 7

3 weeks later: Somewhere in the Middle East

"Grant, it's Alexander."

The satellite phone connection crackled, the result of a lightning storm causing local ionization. But Grant could tell it was his brother on the other end of the line.

"That lead we were chasing down just panned out. We finally know who took her. "

"Tell me."

"Sheikh Samir Ben Alid."As Grant listened to Alex report, the blood froze in his veins. Samir Ben Alid was a lover not a killer. But he was also ruthless and a vindictive son of a bitch. Unfortunately Grant knew he thought he had something to be vindictive about. However if he had hurt Amanda, Grant intended to pay him back in kind.

"Grant, are you still there?"

"Yes."

"Taking on the Ben Alid's is not going to be an easy task."

"Yes, I know."

"Tatianna and I will pull a rescue team together and will be there in the next forty-eight hours."

"Thanks Alex. I owe you one."

"No, you don't. What is family for?"

The line cut off, and Grant lay back on the bed. He was averaging three hours of sleep a night, and his body was exhausted. If he was to rescue Amanda, he had to be at his best, physically as well as mentally. He knew Alex, if he said forty-eight hours, his brother would be there in forty-seven hours and fifty-nine minutes, no more, no less. In the meantime, Grant needed to sleep, but he knew there was no sleep to be had. Instead, he pulled out his chair and started dismantling and cleaning his Glock 42.

***

"AMANDA, I'M SO GLAD you joined us," Samir said, standing and helping her with her seat before sending Yusef away.

"Us?"

Before Samir could answer, a young woman stepped through the dining hall doors. She was gorgeous, prettier by far than any of the other women in the harem, even Nadia, with dark brown hair that hung around her face in loose curls, and warm brown eyes that sparkled with a heady combination of warmth and seduction. Like the others she was thin with proportions that would leave most men on their knees, begging for attention. A woman like that would live in men's fantasies until their dying day, she was sure, and the merest whisper of her lips upon a man's flesh would melt his will to her every whim.

The young woman was dressed in Western fashion, jeans and a spaghetti-strap top, showing off the amazing hourglass figure of her body and highlighting her breasts, which were almost too perky to be believed. Sighing, Amanda covered her own curvier bust as best she could with her coral blue silk top. Amanda knew that only a couple of weeks ago she would have felt like nothing compared to this girl who really couldn't have been more than twenty. But she had grown quite a bit in the last few weeks. She had taken her rightful place as one of the women in the harem, and she knew the Sheikh desired her as much if not more than the other beauties. Maybe even more, as he hadn't slept with anyone in the harem ever since she arrived. She was currently the harem favorite. Despite knowing better she could not help being flattered. What woman wouldn't?

Samir surprised her by narrowing his eyes at the newcomer. "Jasmine, you can't wear that out later today."

The girl laughed and swept her long, dark locks back over her shoulders the back flowing down almost to her waist. "How many times must I tell you, Samir? I am not going to live by those ancient rules any more. You can thank your sending me to Paris for university for my lack of appreciation of traditional Islamic culture, but I find nothing wrong with my body. You can control others, but you also know I think it's your biggest fault." The young woman turned her gaze to Amanda, her mouth breaking open in a grin. "You're Amanda, right? He never shuts up about you."

Amanda blinked. This was certainly interesting. She had never seen anyone stand up to Samir before, and get away with it. "Oh, I...who are you?"

Jasmine leaned across the massive table so that she could shake her hand. "I'm his kid sister Jasmine, you know, the one he can't boss around and shouldn't worry about what I wear."

The tightness in Amanda's chest eased. "It's nice to meet you. But I must agree with your brother. If you wear that, well, it's like 120 degrees here. You're going to burn your skin to a crisp."

"Jasmine has to be appropriate in front of others. For the guards and for all other men, she has to have her body covered and she knows this," Samir said as if by rote, then his demeanor softened and he winked at his little sister. "However, I'll excuse your attire for now so when we see your surprise, you can be more comfortable."

"Thanks. You're the only brother I have who really gets me."

"I thought that was why you freeloaded," Samir joked.

The servant who came out this time was a small woman who continued to refill their coffee and also brought a platter of grilled lamb and various vegetables. Amanda's stomach growled and she dug in, relishing the tastes of turmeric that exploded on her tongue. While Samir had more than once provided her with what he called "American food," she had come to enjoy Middle Eastern cuisine as well.

"Big brother, I'm the most interesting guest you have," Jasmine replied, and then smiled genuinely back at Amanda. "Okay, second most. I like this one. She's got spunk."

"You're flattering Miss Granger because you want to go to America and will probably suggest she shoves you in her luggage for later."

"No, well, okay, but she's still more fun than the other girls. They just sip coffee and glare at me."

Amanda smiled, a bit taken aback by how forward she was. "I

41

will sip the coffee, it's amazing. If I ever go home to America, you can come visit me. I don't think that'll be for a while. I need to get over this pesky memory loss first, but I bet you'd love New York or L.A."

"Oh Hollywood!" she said, standing and twirling about. "I could be a movie star anytime. That's my biggest goal!"

Samir shook his head. "Last week she wanted to be a doctor. Two weeks ago a dressage horse riding champion. She'll want to be a fighter pilot next week."

Jasmine nodded. "I intend to do everything that I can in life. It's really the only way to live. Isn't that right, Amanda?"

"I think so," she said, coughing and sipping more coffee. God, if this girl only knew the new experiences that Amanda had been having in her brother's harem. *Unless these experiences aren't new?*

"I can't agree more," Samir purred, grinning back at her and, damn it, her panties were wet again already. Samir had been a gentleman after that first messed up dinner, but in his eyes smoldered a desire and promise of pleasure that left her aroused almost constantly.

The trio ate their lunch with gusto, Amanda feeling comfortable as the diminutive Jasmine ate almost as much as she did. Samir wiped his lips with a napkin after his last skewer of lamb, and stood up. "So, Jasmine, would you like to see your surprise?"

She grinned. "Again? Father is right, you spoil me."

"Well it's more fun to spoil you than our brothers," he replied, standing. He offered Amanda a crooked elbow and she took it.

They walked arm and arm like that through the palace's labyrinthine corridors until reaching a gorgeous garden. It reminded her of the hanging gardens of Babylon she'd read about in history class. There was greenery everywhere, and even now, sprinklers were running to keep it lush. There were hydrangeas, lilacs, things that couldn't possibly grow here, but that must have needed a massive staff just to cultivate. The roses were exceptional, not just a deep blood red but also white and midnight purple. There were no thorns on any of them.

In the center of this garden was a beautiful Arabian stallion with a mane as dark as coal. He was held on a lead line by another female servant and Amanda grinned at his actions. However he'd done it, probably text message, maybe with just the power of his personality, Samir had kept his word so that his sister could be comfortable in clothing she preferred. She didn't have to cover up with only female servants around.

It was a sweet concession for his sister, and it made Amanda appreciate his heart and dedication all the more.

When Jasmine saw the horse she squealed and ran toward him. "He's amazing!"

From back by the rose bushes, Samir laughed. "Tornado isn't broken in completely yet. When I've finished taming him, he'll be yours. If you want to follow your passion for dressage, you should become the best. The only way to be the best is to ride the best. And with Tornado, you have a mount worthy of an Olympic champion."

She smiled at both of them and bowed low. "Thank you, brother." Jasmine wandered off with Tornado, the servant holding the stallion's lead, the young woman running her hands over his mane and neck.

CHAPTER 8

Amanda and Samir stood together, alone in the rose garden, her thoughts swirling. It had been weeks since the failed seduction attempt. Since then Samir had been extremely patient, happy to go at her pace.

She had to admit she could have never imagined sharing a man with other women, but in the last couple of weeks Samir had poured all his attention on her. His courtship was intoxicating. It had her toying with the idea of them together. *Emma would tell me to stop being delusional.*

The thought came unbidden to her mind, leaving her swirling in confusion. Who was Emma?

As Amanda tried to recapture the memory it flitted away. She took a deep breath and decided to focus on the now, instead of on a past that kept eluding her. Whatever feelings she had for Samir didn't change the fact that she was living in a gilded cage, and he was her prison master. But was she willing to give herself to him, knowing fully that he was likely to dump her for the next beauty as soon as she did? *The best case, I get a couple of months of his attention.*

Samir took a knife from his pocket and cut the biggest red rose for her. "Please, for you. It is not as gorgeous a color as your hair, but nature can only perfect such a shade once."

"Thanks," she said, taking the flower and sliding it behind her ear. "So what do you do all day here besides sex, buying gifts for your favorite sister, and amusing me?"

"I work a lot. My father and brothers make sure Alid Investments is profitable, while I work hard to ensure it helps others. We donate money to mainly orphanages and hospitals, people hurt by the wars that have torn apart the Middle East for decades."

"That's...wow."

He grinned and kissed her cheek. "You don't think that I can be both a hedonist and a philanthropist at the same time? That's a severe lack of vision, my dear Amanda. I am a man with many facets to my personality."

"You seem to be more than I realized," Amanda said, her voice dropping to almost a whisper level as she spoke her mind openly.

"How so?"

She swallowed her nervousness and started playing with a strand of hair, curling it repeatedly over her forefinger. "I'm just starting to understand that my impression of you was wrong. I think...I think there was a reason why I chose to come here, and that there can be something between us. Clearly, I have fabulous taste."

Samir smiled. In the last three weeks the worry that she would regain her memory had been tormenting him. The lie that kept her docile and in his grasp had been uncomfortable to maintain initially. However the hotter his desire for her burned the easier lying had become. But Amanda intrigued him. Despite being in his possession, somewhere along the road it felt like she possessed him. He had rarely made so many concessions for any other woman.

He hadn't given up on his plan to get back at Hamilton, but it didn't seem as important anymore. He intended to master this woman, like he mastered all under his domain, but lately the willing submission he sought from her seemed less and less important. His need to possess Amanda was becoming an obsession. It was all he could do not to rip her clothes off and ravish her. Her weekly waxing sessions with Nadia were progressing nicely. Amanda's sexual inhibitions were being broken down step by delicious step.

"You do have good taste and I bet you taste even better. Don't judge me from any preconceptions you have about harems. I've had many women, but I have always been looking for the perfect one. The girls come of their own free will, and after they stay in luxury and have access to education and facilities they never could have dreamed of otherwise. Any who wish to go after their initial contract is up is free to. In fact, a few have."

"That's good."

"But I feel it's all practice for the one I truly seek."

Amanda looked down at the rose bushes, at the stems. Was it possible to have everything she wanted? The roses in the garden had no thorns, but could someone as amazing and handsome as Samir have no drawbacks, no hidden strings?

"It all feels so fast," she said, unable to lift her eyes to him.

"Perhaps, but my desire for you burns like an inferno, I cannot wait forever, lest I blaze into nothingness." He looked at her with a feverish intensity. Amanda didn't know what to say. Her traitorous body was humming with need.

"I have a deal for you," Samir said, his voice laced with desire. As he continued to perpetrate the lie of her imprisonment he felt no remorse.

"I am not heartless. I understand that you have no memory of our arrangement. If you are not happy, I am prepared to set you free. I just ask one thing, Amanda."

"What?"

"I would like to spend a night of pleasure with you – see if I can't change your mind about leaving. That being said, I like unusual bed plays. I'm sure by now you can understand that."

"I should?" she riposted. "And what makes you think that?"

He laughed. "Feisty, exactly what I love about you. I won't hurt you, unless you want me to. But really I'm more into pleasure than pain. I just want one night with you to give you more pleasure than you ever imagined possible."

"Big claims," she said looking at him with uncertainty in her eyes.

"I can support them," he said, leaning down and kissing her, his tongue just barely touching her own in a tease. She moaned, her body pressing forward into his embrace. "Give me one night to have my way with you. You only have to say the safe word 'Jade' and I will stop." His grip tightened around her and he fastened his lips passionately against hers. His tongue slipped between her lips and danced around hers, in a sensual feast. When he pulled back she was breathing heavily.

"I want willingness. I might have been too excited at dinner a few weeks ago, but I always respect my bed partners."

"Really?" Amanda said, her breath coming in small gasps. She gulped and pulled back from him a little. "So one night? Anything I want and if it's too much, 'Jade' and I go home."

"You have my word," he said kissing her once more.

When Amanda broke away she was panting, nipples hard with desire. "I will think about it."

As Samir watched her walk away, he knew his conquest was almost complete.

CHAPTER 9

As she dressed for the evening, forgoing the normal hair accessories in favor of a simple flowing of her hair over her shoulder, Amanda wished she had more than five minutes alone to think.

Her body ached with the memory of Samir's touch. The more time she had spent with him, the more she knew that her body craved his touch. Amanda closed her eyes and moaned, her left hand reaching under the soft silk of her top for her breast. She shuddered as her nipple pebbled under her grasp, she was just about to slip inside her panties when she was interrupted by a sharp knock on the door.

Blushing, Amanda stood up and straightened everything, even washed her hands off in the sink for good measure.

A man, kissing her hands, sniffing the arousal left on them. The image drifted unbidden into her mind. Amanda stilled.

Who was that? It wasn't the first time this shadowy figure had emerged from her memories, but every time she tried to remember him clearly the image disappeared.

A part of her had been holding back from sleeping with Samir and somehow she knew the shadowy figure must have something to do with it. Not that she thought Samir was a liar, but what morals can a man have who forces a woman to uphold a deal which involves her providing her body as payment?

The sharp knock on the door persisted.

Any lingering arousal she had was snuffed out like a candle when she found Nadia outside waiting to take her back to the harem's wing.

"Great, what did I do to win the pleasure of your company?" Amanda snapped. This was the last person in the world she wanted to see right now.

Nadia's answering smirk made Amanda want to slap her; the other woman didn't have the right to look like she'd just won the lottery. "Samir wanted someone to give you extra attention on the way back, in case you stumbled. I volunteered."

"Like he believes you would help me."

Nadia shrugged and leaned in, her breath caressing Amanda's neck. "I have such things to show you, *little* girl. You need to learn your place," she whispered in her ear, causing Amanda to shudder in mixed revulsion and remembered desire. It didn't matter, she would never like Nadia, no matter how many orgasms the bitch in heat gave her. Moving back, Nadia glanced into the room on the left. "You wait there. I have one file to grab from Dr. Assad."

Amanda forced herself to smile. She knew that it was now or never. Her decision was made.

Regardless of how much Samir excited her, regardless of the opulence and the luxury, she had to be free. No father worth his salt would sell his daughter in bondage to save himself. And if hers would, then he wasn't worth saving. She could not be another bird in this beautiful gilded cage, even if freedom was dangled before her as a prize. Freedom was priceless. She felt overwhelmed with sadness that he did not understand. The mere fact he had dangled it as a carrot in front of her meant she had to leave this place as soon as she could. *I wasn't raised to be a man's property.*

It wasn't that, at some level, she didn't want to explore more with Samir. God, the way she ached for him told her the opposite. Despite her body riding her hard in this place, which seemed to be built for decadent pleasure she wasn't completely stupid. She couldn't make a decision of such importance when she didn't know who she was. Who was the shadowy man in her memories? Somehow she knew it was important for her to remember, before it was too late.

It would take very little for her to fall completely for Samir, to even accept this lifestyle he offered, where she was one of many. Despite Nadia's sadistic games, it was because of her heart she was planning to run away. Samir's words and actions were as contradictory as her desire for him was self-evident. If she didn't get away soon, she would never leave. She couldn't give up her freedom, regardless of the pleasure. As remorse and loss at the thought of leaving Samir behind coursed through her veins, she turned and looked innocently at Nadia.

"How would I get anywhere? I'm too fat to make any real distance, isn't that right?"

"Typical overfed American," Nadia sneered and she turned. It gave Amanda the opportunity she had been waiting for.

The second Nadia wasn't looking Amanda linked the fingers of her left and right hands together over her head and slammed her joined hands down hard on Nadia's skull. The woman collapsed to the floor with a thud, and Amanda was off, sprinting down the hallway.

She wasn't sure how long she had until Nadia woke up and ran for her. God, she wasn't even sure if Dr. Assad would figure it out and call for the guards with their choice of scary weapons. All she knew as she rushed down the halls and toward what she hoped was a main door between the wings was she needed to escape while the coast was clear.

As Amanda rounded the corner, she wished she had kept up with her exercise. Damn it, she was getting a cramp. Rushing through the halls, the marble beneath her was slick and her bare feet weren't finding stable purchase. As she hurried toward that large bejeweled door before the wide spiral staircase that she prayed hard to be the entry foyer, she slipped. Her legs shot out in front of her, and she went sliding, the silk of her pants reducing the friction to the point she looked like a baseball player going for a stolen base, as she slid directly into Samir, who was rounding the corner coming the other direction.

Breathing heavily, she got to her hands and knees and started babbling. "I can explain. I...Samir, Nadia's being a bitch … I .. I mean it's not what it looks like."

Beautiful and soft gray eyes looked into hers as lean strong arms picked her up. The ease with which he lifted her up made her mouth water. The sane part of her mind groaned disapprovingly.

Samir frowned back at her and stroked her hair back from her face. Despite herself, she leaned into the embrace. "I don't understand. Where's Yusef?"

"I---"

She wasn't able to finish as Nadia, flanked by the two large guards and Yusef, trotted up to them.

Samir dropped his hand from her face and turned toward the other woman. "What happened? Amanda says you threatened her."

"Hardly," Nadia barked. "The *sha*...American attacked me and tried to flee the compound."

"I didn't mean to attack her I was just trying to get away!" Amanda shouted before she could stop and think. As soon as she did, a deathly pallor fell over her face, and her hands clapped over her mouth. Silence fell and you could have heard a hairpin drop.

"Master Alid, one of the harem's cardinal rules is you shall do no harm to your sisters," Nadia said, looking up at Samir with eagerness in her eyes. "She's dangerous, Master Alid. She needs to be disciplined for her transgression."

Samir nodded his head and passed Amanda to Yusef's care. There was a spark of some unidentifiable emotion in his eyes. "We cannot have any woman in the harem attacking the others. This must be punished, but I am not sending Amanda away." His voice cold, his next words bore the steely tones of command. "Nadia, I expect you to undertake the necessary discipline. I don't want a mark on her however." Sighing, Samir kissed her forehead and walked away.

"Punishment?" Amanda repeated in a dazed voice. Could he be serious? What had happened to her beautiful sheikh?

"You can't let her do this!" she shouted to Samir's retreating figure. It was at that precise moment Amanda realized she had nothing to bargain with.

Nadia looked at her with a smug smile. "Yes, Master," she said to Samir's back, before turning to Amanda and smiling with satisfaction, her voice dropping to where just the two of them could hear. "Don't worry, American. I promise to take really good care of you."

Two guards emerged on each side and started dragging Amanda away. "Samir! Samir! Please!!!!" As Amanda's screams echoed through the halls the sheikh was nowhere to be seen.

CHAPTER 10

Amanda found herself stark naked, strung up, her arms and legs each tied with black silk scarves to the posts of a four poster bed. Scared, she could only begin to imagine what her current position would mean for her punishment. The bed was luxurious, as soft a mattress as she'd ever felt, with rich yellow and orange fabric hanging from its posts. Around her there were pillows, rugs, and more candles than she could count. The wall to her right was almost floor to ceiling mirrors, starting just a few inches off the ground and continuing almost all the way to the ceiling. The air hung thick with the scents of frankincense and jasmine.

The opulence of her surroundings only increased Amanda's fear. If this luxurious room was supposed to be used for her punishment, what strange ideas did Samir have in mind?

The door to her left opened, and Yusef entered, wearing only loose black flowing pants, cinched and tied at the waist and the ankles with silken cords. She gulped. There was no way Samir would let Yusef touch her, would he? Relief washed over her momentarily as Yusef stepped to the side, crossing his arms over his powerful chest. Behind him however was Nadia, and Amanda felt a mixture of ire mingled with relief of the familiar. Yusef stood by the door, guarding the exit, while Nadia set her two boxes on the pillows below the bed. It was clear who the punisher was going to be.

"Why are you doing this?" Amanda spat out. "Where is Samir?"

"Where the Master is, is none of your business," Nadia replied, her voice was thick with danger and something else, something Amanda couldn't quite understand. She made quick work of setting everything else up, taking off her own top and pants until she stood there naked save for a translucent black thong. "In addition to punishment, this is also a lesson for you, girl. Today's lesson is all about pleasure and submission, the things you have to truly know if you ever hope of pleasing our master."

"I... where is he?"

"That's for us to know, not you," Nadia said, picking up a glass bottle of oil from the smaller box.

"Yusef, give her the tonic." Amanda watched helplessly as Yusef approached her. She knew it was pointless to fight him. Either she drank the liquid or they were going to force it down her throat. Seething with rage she forced her lips open and swallowed the concoction without protest.

Somewhere overhead, instrumental music, slow and seductive, with lots of rich woodwinds and soft tones began playing, making the whole room seem even more like a scene of seduction instead of punishment. The oil smelled heavily of nutmeg and warmed Amanda's skin almost as soon as Nadia's hands touched her skin.

Her first touch was on Amanda's right shoulder, and Amanda stiffened. After weeks of Nadia's special treatment she knew there must be something else in those lotions, something aphrodisiac.

Nadia's skilled fingers worked their way over her shoulders and neck, kneading out the knots that stress had built there. Clamping her lips shut, Amanda couldn't deny the pleasure that was starting to radiate from her skin. She was used to Nadia's touch, and her traitorous body was associating whatever was to come with the forbidden pleasures Nadia had already delivered on her body. She blushed, but any shame was quickly forgotten as Nadia moved lower. Her hands, still covered with the aromatic oil, trailed over her breasts. For once in her life, Amanda was glad she was voluptuous, and could feel the other woman's hands as they lingered over her nipples and round curves. Nadia's talented hands tickled at first, just little touches. Unable to hold it back any longer, Amanda mewled and bucked her hips as best as she could, despite the constraints.

Even as her mind screamed no, her body betrayed her, and her mouth opened, a quiet sigh escaping. "You have probably guessed this from last time. The oils I am using are an ancient ointment used for the arousal of reluctant brides and harem girls." Nadia grinned. "Combined with the liquid you just drank, soon you will be begging to be fucked."

Nadia smirked at her and started twisting and teasing her nipples, working them up to full, erect arousal. Both stood peaked stiff, as the slim woman ran her tongue over Amanda's left nipple, using all of her skills to tease and taste the American's creamy skin. She started with tiny bites, the pressure measured just enough to entice but not hurt, causing Amanda to cry out in pleasure. Nadia pulled her head away far too quickly, but kept her left hand teasing her captive's nipple. The other hand continued its ministrations with the oil, trailing over her hips and then caressing her thighs.

"You," Nadia hissed, her voice deeper than usual, "are actually very beautiful, my *habibi*. It is too bad there is so much of you though."

Amanda's cheeks flamed. "Maybe if you had some nutrients in you, I wouldn't have kicked your ass. And don't call me *habibi*!" It was an endearment she only ever wanted to hear from Samir.

Where was Samir? Why would he leave her to this torture? Every breath felt laborious, every touch burned. Desire was flowing like molten lava through her veins, her every sense heightened and attuned to pleasure. Amanda started writhing in her bonds. Her body demanded delicious release and she knew she could not win this battle. Her inner muscles were tightening, aching for some sort of release. She couldn't... she needed...she, "Please make me come!" she groaned. Any embarrassment at the knowledge that Yusef was watching her being sexually punished was lost in the tidal wave of her need.

Nadia removed her hand, causing Amanda to whimper at the loss of her touch. "I thought you'd never ask."

The slim woman stepped out of sight, and for a minute Amanda thought that Yusef might step in. Amanda was so aroused she didn't care, she just needed her body filled. Her clit was throbbing, her juices running part way down her leg and her body sensitized like a thousand little jolts of electricity running all over her. Someone had to make her come and now.

"Yusef. The strap-on." The guard who had so far stood stoically reached within one of the boxes and withdrew a doublepronged dildo. The harness fitted like a pair of panties the only sign of its purpose a penis like protrusion on the inside attached to a bigger phallus protruding on the outside. Amanda watched as Yusef pulled the panties up along her legs. Nadia held on to his large bulging arms as she stepped into the strap-on. He pumped the end in and out of her until she was panting hard and her juices had properly lubricated the toy. The vision of him spreading Nadia's pussy fold to insert the dildo into her cleft had Amanda juicing even harder and wishing that was her.

As Nadia finally positioned the toy by inserting it fully in her own wet tunnel she turned to Yuself and said, "Thank you. You may leave us now." With no additional prompt Yusef walked out of the room. The only betrayal of his interest was the bulging erection in his pants.

Nadia turned with the harness strapped around her waist. She leaned in close to Amanda's ear, whispering words that Amanda knew were meant only for her. "As I told you before. You're going to be mine. Even before the Master, I'm going to be the one who your body yearns for. As I yearn for yours." Despite the fog of desire that had descended over her, Amanda finally understood. Nadia's desire for her was similar to Samir. This exotic woman wasn't a twenty-four hour bitch because she was mean, but to disguise the very real desire she had for women. Even as the realization dawned on her, Amanda knew she would not have cared whatever the reason was. Her body now craved satisfaction and she desperately needed Nadia and her strap-on to fuck her to blissful release.

Nadia positioned herself between Amanda's legs, the jutting blue cock sticking out from her groin. The molten avalanche of desire that coursed through her veins made Amanda yearn for her possession. She accepted the position, opening her thighs as much as her restraints would let her, her eyes beckoning. Desire now overshadowing any sense of embarrassment or shame. "Nadia. Fuck me, please," Amanda groaned.

The tortured words caused Nadia to pause her actions, her head tilted to the side. Nadia stalked across the room, untying one of Amanda's legs before throwing it in the air and over her shoulder, the position both spreading her open wider and hiding part of Nadia's face from the mirror's view. "Your desire is my pleasure, *habibi*," she mouthed, as she lined up the vibrating dildo with the entrance to Amanda's pussy. "Know that as I fuck you until you scream in blissful release, our Master likely watches through the mirror with great enjoyment."

"Then we better give him a show that makes him regret he is not with us," Amanda said, her voice dripping with physical need. Her clit throbbed mercilessly and she knew she was ready to beg for it, on her knees if she could.

"Ask me again." Nadia replied, her lips that were hidden by Amanda's calf and foot, forming a smile even as she kept her eyes hard and unforgiving.

The stimulation of the dildo was so intense Amanda started to cry, she needed release. Sobbing she begged, "Please Nadia, I am sorry I hit you, please FUCK ME."

With a satisfied smile Nadia pushed forward, spreading open Amanda's tight walls, the vibrations causing Amanda to cry out in pleasure as her empty, aching body was filled. The dildos vibrations coursed through her body, causing her to buck her hips forward, trying to get more of it inside her. Nadia held herself there for at least a minute, keeping her on the edge, but not letting her get enough stimulation to actually come.

Amanda lost herself in the cascade of emotions, sobbing. "Please, Nadia. Please take me all the way. I'm begging you."

Nadia's hands reached around to hold Amanda's hips, pushing herself in fully. Amanda groaned.

"Yes, it pleases me," Nadia replied in a husky voice. Although the larger end of the dildo was in Amanda the other end was firmly wedged in her pussy, making her juices flow. "Now, you will feel it all." She started moving her hips back and forth, pumping the dildo in and out of Amanda's soaked tunnel.

With each forward thrust, the base of the strap on would nudge against her clit, causing the redhead to cry out in delight. Her nub was so swollen. She raised her own hips as best as she was able and fucked back against the strap-on with reckless abandon. The air was alive with the scent of the two women, incense, and spiced oil. The feeling of Nadia inside her, while her hidden hand surreptitiously stroked her inner thigh tenderly had every nerve ending in her body on fire. She stroked her fingers on her clit, pinching it gently, giving Amanda the last bit she needed. She came, her entire body quaking as she screamed, loud enough that the entire harem could have heard her.

Nadia pumped harder, relishing the fact she was both fucking Amanda and fucking herself at the same time. She orgasmed shortly after. She immediately took off her harness and dildo before cleaning herself up in a brief, businesslike fashion. Reaching below Amanda's line of sight, she drew out a pair of underwear, curiously cut into a boyshort configuration that to Amanda looked somehow thick or stiff. Pushing her legs together, Nadia worked the panties up and onto Amanda's hips. Amanda felt a round cylinder object inserted into her pussy. Looking her in the eyes, her face turned away from the mirror, she saw Nadia mouth "sorry" before pulling them on fully. She then turned and left without a backwards glance.

Amanda lay on the bed, exhausted and sexually satiated, wondering what Nadia meant with her apology. Then a soft humming sound started from the panties, the vibrations coursing through Amanda's clit, centering on the cylinder at the entrance of her tunnel, and she couldn't think at all.

CHAPTER 11

From behind his mirror, Samir watched everything unfold. He had instructed Nadia weeks ago to break down Amanda's sexual inhibitions. He should have guessed she would have chosen this particular punishment. His conscience was nagging him about the need to resort to tricks to get Amanda's consent. *I should stop this.*

He was reaching for the intercom button when Nadia pulled out the oils and his finger dropped away, traveling instead to the waistband of his pants, finding his belt. Alone in his viewing room, Samir opened his pants and grabbed his cock. Once he saw Nadia's hands on such round and willing flesh, he'd lost control, masturbating like he hadn't since he was a teenager.

He tried his best to keep a slow pace; to give himself the maximum pleasure he could from the erotic sight in front of him as his two favorite women shared pleasure. When Nadia stood up to put on the strap on, his eyes were slitted against the pressure building inside him, his breath coming in grunts and gasps. As

Nadia's dildo had spread open the soft pink lips of Amanda's pussy, his hand sped up, pumping hard, fingers sliding over his sensitive head with lightning speed as the precum slickened his hand.

The still minute, as Nadia held herself inside Amanda, not moving, were torture for him. Especially as he saw Amanda's face flush, the pinkness spreading over her creamy skin almost all the way to her breasts, but he held back the pumping of his own hand until Nadia started her thrusts. His eyes closing as he imagined himself buried inside Amanda's long desired wetness, his cock spreading her open and causing her to cry out the way she was in the other room.

When Amanda came, screaming so loud he didn't even need the intercom to hear her wails, her fiery hair cascading over her face, he reached his limit, his cock spewing over the window and wall, soaking his hand and even his pants, leaving him gasping with his forehead pressed against the glass, trembling in exertion.

Part of him envied Nadia. He had wanted to explore the sensual depths of Amanda's body first, to be the first to spread her open in such a fashion and cause her to cry out so. He wondered if she would scream the same way for him. He didn't know, couldn't imagine such pleasures, but damn it if he wasn't going to find out.

As he walked out of the viewing room and straight to the pleasure room where Amanda was still bound only one thought was on his mind. He would be denied no longer.

***

THE SILK CLOTH WAS tight against Amanda's wrists. Sensitive

from her recent orgasm the vibrating panties were torture, her clit soon throbbing with renewed need. Did he enjoy what he saw? Was he pleased? All she wanted right now was for him to be please so he could release her from her heavenly torture. Her mind could barely focus, with the painful pleasure rippling from the panties on her clit, but thoughts kept swirling in her head.

Three weeks ago she would have denied it was possible she enjoyed what had just transpired, but in this world of heady desires she had finally discovered a side of herself she hadn't been aware off. The thought of Samir deriving pleasure from watching her sexual surrender had her juicing. She wanted him to have enjoyed what he had seen her and Nadia do. Never had she yearned so desperately to submit to another's sexual desires. Even as the words swirled in her mind she knew she sounded insane. As waves of painful desire continued to wash over her she fervently hoped he would come for her. In the aftermath she still ached. An ache she knew she needed Samir to soothe. She didn't know how much more stimulation she would be able to take before she burst into tears from the intensity of it all. As if materialized by her feverish mind, she heard the door open and he walked in. Tall, dark, and dangerous.

She licked her lips and felt heat flare in her pussy. He was delicious. Wild, untamed black hair flowing freely out of its confines and curling about his shoulders. He wore nothing now and she could appreciate the muscles of his abs, the dip in his hips where she could see the flesh curve around bone.

It was funny. She'd never really understood the point of calling something a happy trail, but she did now. The thin line of dark hair that teased down from his belly button to the black swath over his groin, only fueled her fantasies of kissing her way down it until she enveloped him with her mouth.

She swallowed at the thought. She didn't think she was that much into oral before, even in her fantasies about him since their deal. Now that she saw his erection springing free however, the girth of him and pink head, wet already with precum, Amanda wanted all of him. To please him with everything she had.

"I have not come to ask you for permission. I will not stop." His voice was thick with both promise and threat.

"I don't want you to!" she whispered back, desire making her voice husky. "I am yours, Samir, willingly. Please take me."

"As you wish," he replied. Reaching over, he picked up the remote for the vibrating pants and pressed a button, the speed increased so fast and dizzying that Amanda thought she'd pass out, the pleasure overwhelming her was so vast. Just when she thought she would pass out from overload he turned it off. With trembling hands he caressed her thighs and slowly pulled the vibrating panties off of her. They were soaking wet. Her clit was engorged and her vagina lips puffy. As he lightly caressed the entrance to her tunnel he whispered, "I wish I was the one to fuck you so hard your pussy got this deliciously swollen." Amanda moaned as every light caress sent bolts of electricity through her body. Her stomach tightened.

"This will not be over quickly," Samir warned with a voice thick with desire. "But you will enjoy every moment of it."

With no warning he spread her thighs apart, and thrust his cock hard inside her. She felt a jolt as he buried himself all the way to the hilt, pain only avoided because she had been so aroused for so long.

He was slightly curved, throbbing, stretching her pussy to the point she was crying in pleasure even before he started to pump.

The curve of his cock rubbed against all the pleasurable points inside her, making the vibrating panties seem like a mild forgotten memory.

"For too long, I have yearned to bury myself deep inside you," he muttered through gritted teeth. Deep satisfaction colored his features. His cock throbbing inside her, Samir leaned forward and untied her arms. "I want you with me too." Amanda nodded, wrapped her arms around his neck, moving her hips as well as she could in time as he started to pump into her wet sheath in deep hard thrusts. His curved tool was plowing through her tender parts mercilessly. Again and again. Maybe the man wasn't human.

That had to be it, she was sure.

He was a devil, an incubus sent to tempt her and Amanda wanted him to. She was more than ready to surrender to the flame of desire that burned between them, regardless of the cost or outcome. Pleasure mingled with pain, and where one started and the other ended was impossible to say.

She was sure she had never felt this way before.
A shadowy image of a man in an Armani suit flittered through her mind.

Samir kissed her, tongue fierce and hungry, while one hand played skillfully with her nipple as his cock filled her again and again.

She was sure she had never known submission like this before.
A shadowy image of a man deliciously spanking her floated through her mind. Amanda stilled in confusion.

Samir pinned her down to the bed, lavishing her sensitive breast with his tongue. As he continued to pump her wet tunnel relentlessly full of cock, she was soon lost to anything but the delicious satisfaction of submission.

Amanda felt like her mind was being ripped in two, as fragments of memories overlaid with the pleasure of Samir inside her, echoing each other, the pleasure of each magnifying the other to the point she wasn't sure which was the memory and which was real.

Before she could recapture her memories the stimulation was too much. Amanda's thoughts were again obliterated as Samir thrust himself with intensity and passion. She screamed as he filled her again and again, pleasuring her body with his curved cock. She wanted to come, but still Samir had not let her, until she begged, her voice harsh with lust. "Please, make me come, Master Alid."

"Only after I come," Samir replied, his breath coming in short little grunts as he reached up and grasped her nipple with his fingers. He pinched the hard little nub just as his pelvis rubbed against her pussy, sending stars shooting through her vision. The clenching of her pussy around his cock triggered his release, and he bellowed, his thick seed filling her body with the pleasure and permission she had sought. She surrendered herself fully to the sensations, her own screams of climax harmonizing with his, until she collapsed on the bed, exhausted.

For long minutes Amanda lay stunned by what they had just done. She didn't think it was her imagination, although with the sensations running through her she couldn't be sure. But as he had pinched her nib, and she felt the first twitches of his orgasm in her pussy, he had grunted one simple phrase that echoed through her mind:

"I will never give you up."

EPILOGUE

Grant looked at the scattered pictures and felt bile rising in his throat. The evidence was irrefutable. Amanda with Sheikh Samir Ben Alid. Hand in hand, looking for all the world like a romantic couple in love.

The part of him that had sent men crying out of his boardroom was roaring in his ears.

She wouldn't, she hadn't. Not when he had been frantically scouring the world looking for her.

No, he would not believe she had left him of her own free will. This had to be a clever montage.

Whatever the truth he was going to wring the life out of Samir, very slowly.

Determined he turned towards the assault team assembled by his brother.

"Tatianna should have her by now. Get ready for the signal." He cocked his Glock and walked out of the makeshift tent.

PART 3

CHAPTER 1

Billionaire Tycoon Grant Hamilton, leaned forward against the barrel of his assault gun, and assessed the developing situation with narrow eyes. After scouring the world in search for his kidnapped fiancée, Amanda Cardwell, the moment had finally come to retrieve her from the clutches of her kidnapper. Based on information from Bahrain, Amanda was being held captive by Sheikh Samir Ben Alid, in the desert harem he was currently gazing at.

The Sheikh's secluded estate was built around an unbelievably beautiful oasis. It sprawled over an area extending further than 20 miles. The shade of the trees nearest the pool served as a resting place, created around stunning, lush gardens.

In terms of any real fortress like protection, it had none. Whilst the gardens and trees created seclusion and intimacy, they also obscured any view of approaching enemies.

Currently, a pair of six-man teams were scattered around the parameter awaiting Grant's orders. The men had been instructed to only shoot to kill if they absolutely had to. Hopefully, this rescue would never come to that.

More comfortable in the boardroom than on a mission that involved storming a guarded desert harem, Grant would not have been anywhere else than at the forefront of this assault. Snapping out of his musing he glanced up and noted the approaching dark, swirling clouds, moving steadily in their direction.

"I think luck is about to be our lady tonight."

"Really?" his brother Alexander replied, moving forward to get into a better position to cover the estate.

"Yes, it's another four hours until sundown, but with the overhanging clouds we will be able to execute the rescue plan in the next 20 minutes."

"I know you want to get to her as quickly as possible but I still think we need to give Tatianna more time inside the harem to locate her."

"We are going in as soon as the sky is overcast." Grant replied, his voice cold and uncompromising.

Alex took a deep breath. Although he worked for Uncle Sam as a spy and a sniper, he had relinquished control of the rescue operation from the onset to his brother. No one could argue with Grant when he had made his mind up. He was in his Louis VII mood as their mother called it. Still, he had to try.

"You are making this personal," he commented with a frown.

Grant continued to look at the dark mass emerging in the sky overhead, a dark storm to mirror the anger coursing through his veins. He remembered the blood on the note left for him. Emotions that had been bottled up since the kidnapping, started rising to the surface. Determined he stomped them down. He turned and looked at his brother.

"Samir Ben Alid made this personal when he abducted Amanda. I am not going to pretend. I want to wring the living daylights out of him, and pummel him to a pulp." His gaze reverted to the estate.

Alex sighed inwardly and thanked God he had better control of his emotions. "Be that as it may, this all seems a bit too easy," he replied. "I can't imagine that we've gotten this far and haven't set off any hidden alarms."

"What the hell are you trying to say?" Grant retorted, without removing his observation for one second, from the sprawling oasis estate.

"I don't know. I have a bad feeling," Alex replied, giving his brother a humorless smile.

Grant rubbed his temples, eyes still firmly fixed on the target. "I know what you mean. The trail from Bahrain that led us straight to Samir's door step seemed a bit too easy."

"Perhaps we should pull back, regroup, and negotiate Ben Alid's surrender," Alex suggested.

Grant shook his head. "It's not like you to be this apprehensive. I thought you were the big shot, super spy?"

"Well, I used to not give a damn," Alex said. "Now I've got a wife who at this very moment is infiltrating an enemy camp without me at her back."

"You are lucky Tati isn't here to hear you say any of this. She would kick your uptight behind."

"She would definitely try," Alex muttered and they both burst out laughing.

When Grant had met his new sister in-law, a couple of days earlier, a misplaced comment had her flipping him over on his ass. Tatianna Romanovsky Hamilton was an ex Russian Internal

3

Security Agent. She looked like a curvaceous bombshell, but was deadly as hell. He was not about to underestimate her, or her skills again.

For two days, they had been waiting for the perfect opportunity for Tatianna to infiltrate the harem. When pictures had been taken of Samir and Amanda running around like two lovebirds Grant had almost ordered the men to storm the place. But the nerves of steel that served him well in the boardroom had ensured he stuck to the original plan.

It was well known in the area that Ben Alid was planning an opulent party and feast in the coming days. This meant a lot of unknown people walking into and out of the oasis estate. Despite the almost non-existing security, a stealth approach was the most prudent strategy. Tati had slipped in completely un-noticed, covered from head to toe, pretending to be part of the catering team. *Infiltration, extraction,* and hopefully *zero loss of life.*

Grant mulled over the risks of the operation as he looked through the scope of his AK47 rifle. Through the window of the east wing of the estate, a young woman was dancing. Her movements showed passion and joy. She was surrounded by other women, who were watching and clapping in encouragement. Yes, the risks were clear and present. If anything went horribly wrong not only Amanda, but also these innocent women might get hurt.

A tremor went through his body and for a split second, rage flowed, hot and pure, unmasked by his usual business veneer. Those who knew the Hamilton brothers always assumed that Grant was the calm, cool, collected one. Only Alex and Chase knew that sometimes, that veneer cracked, and the rage that poured out was lethal.

One day in middle school some older, rich punk had beaten up Chase and stolen his Sony Walkman. Grant had found Alex holding their younger, bloodied brother. Although he had no clear memory of what happened next, apparently he had made them take him to the boy, and given him such a bad beating it required three people to get him off of the poor student. The boy had ended up spending a week in the hospital and Grant had almost been thrown out of the boarding school. Luckily enough, Hamilton money had ensured that hadn't happened.

Ever since that day, Grant's emotions were always kept in check. He did not do anything on impulse. That was until he had set his eyes on Amanda Cardwell.

Although he didn't believe in love at first sight, now in retrospect he realized that was exactly what had happened. She had stolen his heart with one smile. The knowledge that he had put her in danger ate away at him, the demon of rage riding him hard.

Suddenly a figure emerged from the east corner of the grounds. It was Tatianna Hamilton, and she had Amanda in tow. They were making a run for it to the far end of the estate where the Sheikh kept his prized vehicles. Hot on their trail were men dressed in black from head to toe.

Men that did not belong to the harem's guard team, and shouldn't have been there at all. Somehow, something else was afoot, beside the covert rescue operation. Grant frowned. The men were gaining on the women.

He squeezed the trigger of his rifle and one of the men fell with a heavy thud. Even as Grant took the shot, Alex's gun went off simultaneously, and the second henchman fell.

Grant dropped his assault weapon, whipped out his pistol and started running. "I am going in," he shouted over his shoulder to his brother.

"I am right behind you," Alex responded grabbing his own handgun, and launched into a full sprint. *All units, stand firm, cover Grant and I,* he instructed over his handheld military radio.

As Grant ran, he knew he was being rash. Better men were at hand for this, but he zig zagged his way down to the estate anyway, trusting Alex and the team to keep the guards and any snipers off of him.

A gunshot rang out. A bullet whizzed past Grant's right shoulder chipping off the bark of a tree he had just veered past.

Heedless of the danger, he continued his sprint.

CHAPTER 2

Sheikh Samir Ben Alid, had four dozen concubines, and frequented some of the most eclectic, bondage dungeons in Europe. He was almost thirty-six, and ruthless in the board room. Ruthless, with everything. Samir Ben Alid did not fall in love. Or at least he thought he didn't. But the anguish he was feeling, at the thought of ever giving up Amanda Cardwell, had to be love.

After their tryst, which lasted through to the early morning, he had been unable to sleep, his mind mulling over the day's events. Amanda had been out like a light, the coupling proving too exhausting for her. As he watched her sleep he was tormented by insecurities.

He wasn't used to worrying about anything. Much less what a woman did, said, or thought. Nevertheless, the knowledge that her memories could separate them left him in an unusual state of anxiety. When had it all changed? When had he decided to keep his flame-haired beauty to himself? As he mused over these questions, he concluded that it did not matter. Ultimately, the memory of her response to his demanding desires, was proof enough that he could still make her his, mind, body and soul. *And mine she shall be.*

Suddenly the revenge he had been after seemed insignificant. Amanda Cardwell was his, and he had no intention of letting her go. He knew she would be disappointed that the freedom he had promised her was not forthcoming. But why would she want to be free after what they had just experienced? There was so much more to explore.

He had not yet completely tamed the defiant flame that burned within her. As much as he thought he loved her, the fantasy he was entertaining, of her complete submission, was even now arousing his manhood. His passions grew darker in tandem with the hardening of his cock. Accustomed to owning and acquiring anything and everything, Samir looked at the opulence that surrounded him, and decide no woman in her right mind would refuse what he had to offer. His mind finally at peace, he decided Amanda might enjoy waking up to his hard possession. The image in his mind made him smile. It was time to wake up his sleeping beauty.

His cell phone rang, shaking him out of his musing. He looked at it, curiosity aroused. Few people had the number to this particular cell, and rare were the occasions it actually rang. With a frown he picked it up and noticed, the callers' number was blocked.

"Hello."

"Samir." The voice was metallic, clearly modified through a digital voice enhancer, but Samir recognized it instantly. It was a voice he had hoped never to hear again.

"What do you want?" he replied.

"Is that anyway to speak to the person, who provided you with the means to get back at the Hamilton's?"

"As I remember, you were compensated handsomely for your 'help,'" Samir responded, steel in his voice. Blinded by his need for revenge he had not questioned the motives, or scruples of the man who had provided him with the means to kidnap Grant Hamilton's bride-to-be.

"Tsk, tsk. Aren't we a bit testy today? Probably has to do with not getting enough sleep. I hope Miss Cardwell isn't keeping you up too late."

"I can't see how that is any of your business."

"Well, I did ensure she was provided to you. It is only good manners to enquire as to how intact she is."

"Whether she is intact or not, is still none of your business."

"Testy, testy. I would have thought you would be in a better mood after spending the night tasting her delights."

Samir gritted his teeth. A game was afoot here that he was missing. It seemed even in his own estate this man had spies. The question was, why? What could he possibly get from that? He mentally took note to review the current security arrangements with Yusef, especially any new additions to the household.

"Get to the point. Why are you calling me? Our business deal was concluded."

"It was indeed, but I thought I would do you one last favor and let you know that a team led by Grant Hamilton is in the process of breaching your walls." The voice sounded smug.

"You really should beef up your security. Any Tom, Dick, and Harry could walk straight into your little harem."

"What the hell does that mean?"

"Don't worry my dear Sheikh, my men are in place to help you deal with this pesky little problem." The line went dead.

Samir stood frozen looking at his phone. If the conversation he had just had meant what he thought it meant every single person on the estate was in grave danger. All he knew of his mysterious caller and benefactor was that he was a very dangerous man. His true name was unknown. He was only referred to as "The Boss" in international crime circles. Not only did he have connections everywhere but he also harbored a deep rooted hatred for the Hamilton's, even greater than the Ben Alid's. If his men had infiltrated the harem, they were at risk. He would not hesitate to gun them all down, for an opportunity to strike a blow at the Hamilton's.

Determined to stop the assault before it began, Samir brought up the number that had just called his cell, and hit redial. After three rings he heard the dreaded message "*This number has not been recognized, please try again or dial another number.*" Frantically he tried the number of the contact that had put him in touch with "The Boss"; the line was dead, as if the number had never existed.

As he stood there, momentarily frozen, he heard a noise. A soft thud against the door, followed by an almost imperceptible shuffling. Fear for his staff and concubines coursed through his veins. He dropped his cell phone, grabbed a decorative scimitar hanging on the wall and dashed to the door. Leaning against the doorframe he unlocked it slowly. With a strong push, he kicked it open and heard a thud as it hit an unknown individual behind the door. Taking a deep breath, scimitar in hand he walked straight into a war zone.

As his gaze surveyed the situation, a cold sensation spread from the pit of his stomach. His guards were engaged in hand-to-hand combat with men dressed from head to toe in black, their faces covered in masks. The fights looked macabre, like silent dances. The only noise that could be heard was grunts and fists pounding flesh. Stunned, Samir stared at the outcome of his desire for revenge. His mind racing, he remembered *Allah* (God) punished those who did wrong. He only hoped today was not the day of his punishment. Yusef and another guard rushed to his side.

"We need to get to the women," he barked to his men. Yusef nodded. Flanking him, they started moving towards the harem section of the estate. As Samir made his way through the hall, kicking and punching through the melee, one thought tormented him. He had to let Amanda go.

CHAPTER 3

Amanda woke up the next morning, lassitude sweeping through her as she thought of the night before. After the incident in the pleasure room, Samir had carried her back to his bedchambers, where they had made love two more times, before they were overtaken by sleep just before dawn.

She glanced around, and saw that Samir had left her a note. "*Habibi*," it began, bringing a smile to her face. "Last night was memorable beyond words. Alas, my family duties fill the day, and I must leave your embrace for a few hours. I shall return by nightfall, to claim you as mine yet again. I have left instructions with Yusef and Nadia that you are to be given free reign of the estate if you so wish. Also, I have instructed that your belongings be moved out of the harem wing. I would have you sleep in my bed from now on." The note was unsigned.

As she lay on the King-size bed, clutching the message and feeling like a giddy little school girl, Amanda's thoughts drifted to the night before. It was all so crazy. The night had been a world-wind of new sensations and experiences. She had discovered a side of herself she hadn't even known she had.

When she had opened her eyes to see Samir towering over her, ready to fulfill all her sexual desires…knowing he had been watching, enjoying their performance for his pleasure. Her only thought had been *please take me*. She would have never imagined, that being forced to submit to another's sexual desires, could be so deliciously erotic and fulfilling. *No wonder I agreed to come to this harem, a place that requires total submission.*

Despite being sore from head to toe, she had to admit she was looking forward to the day to come. *A day spent in Samir's arm*s. Laughing she grabbed one of the pillows and brought it to her face and inhaled. It had Samir's scent lingering on it. Rolling up in bed, still clinging to his pillow, she blinked, realizing it was well past noon. She got to her feet, her legs a bit sore and unsteady. Dressing in Samir's morning gown she made her way to the dining room, where she found another note next to a newspaper. She was flattered that she had brought out the romantic in Samir. Eager she scanned through the words:

PLEASE READ PAGE 15

Perplexed, she picked up the newspaper, to see the New York Times banner atop of the fold. It was out of date by a month or so. Since she hadn't seen a newspaper in her entire time in the estate yet, this mysterious note had her curiosity peaked. Just how was the world doing, in the weeks since she had left it to live here in paradise?

Ignoring the sports and arts section, Amanda turned to the page suggested, which focused on the United States. Her breath caught in her throat. Staring back at her, in stark black and white, was her face, a large smile on her features. *Search For Billionaire's Kidnapped Fiancée Enters Fifth Week*, the headline screamed in bold font. Amanda read on.

"The search for Amanda Cardwell, the fiancée of billionaire, industrial tycoon Grant Hamilton, entered its fifth week today. The dramatic kidnapping has captured the attention of many in high society, not only due to the fairytale nature of their meeting, but also the almost cinematic circumstances surrounding the kidnapping..."

Amanda read the whole story twice. According to it, she had been kidnapped almost six weeks ago, after becoming engaged to Grant Hamilton. While the name tickled something in her mind, her amnesia still prevented her from placing a face to the name. The story continued by saying that after the chief suspect had been arrested, Grant had disappeared, pursuing leads with local authorities around the world trying to find his fiancée. *"Will Amanda Cardwell's fairytale romance have a fairytale ending? This newspaper writer can only pray so."*

The paper dropped to the table as Amanda stared at it numb with shock. She wanted to deny it. It had to be a joke, a bad dream. However, even as the thoughts were forming in her mind, she knew it wasn't so.

Her memories came crashing back to her. How she met Grant, how she spent the day thinking he was a groundskeeper, and still finding him irresistible. The night on the boat, his possession of her body. The engagement, and Natasha's betrayal.

Her hands started to tremble uncontrollably.

With the return of her memories came a flood of emotions. A breathtaking *desire*, a searing *passion*, a *love* forgotten.

"Grant," she moaned, her heart aching.

Her feelings in turmoil she looked around, the opulence surrounding her suddenly appeared to be a gilded cage. She realized an inescapable truth. Her entire relationship with Samir was built on a lie. From the very beginning, the estate was a trap, made to *intoxicate*, *entrance*, and *seduce* her. As she played back yesterday's events, she felt violated. Their lovemaking now reduced to dirty fornication. The sense of betrayal was crippling.

The harem had once made her feel safe, made her believe she was amongst demanding but caring friends. Now she realized it was all an illusion to keep her captive. Had Odella known? Dyana? Dr. Assad? Were they all laughing at how gullible she was? Could they have been so deceitful?

Amanda walked almost catatonically to the bathroom, shedding pieces of clothing as she went. Samir's scent was still on her, clinging to her body. His very seed lingered within her.

What had once been a sign of the pleasures they had shared was now only a reminder of what a fool she had been. As she stood in the shower room, water pouring down removing all traces of his possession, she did not cry.

Once shed of all the physical reminders of her tryst, Amanda made her way to the harem wing of the estate. After entering, she drifted to her bedroom, sitting down on the mattress before placing her head in her hands. *He must have planned this all along. Why would he do this to me? What kind of sick, twisted person kidnaps someone and…and rapes them?*

Even as the thought popped into her head, Amanda knew she was in denial. Samir hadn't raped her, he had made love to her, *seduced* her mind, *conquered* her body. That was the worst betrayal of all. The feelings and memories from last night would forever be with her, reminding her, tormenting her. The very thought of what they had done, and the pleasure she had derived from it, made her feel dirty.

As tears burned behind her eyelids Amanda looked around lost, her mind unable to provide the solace she needed.

CHAPTER 4

She was a prisoner. Her mind repeated the words again, and again, refusing stoutly to give her respite from this undeniable truth. Curled in a fetal position Amanda tried to blank out her inner voice. She needed to think of something, anything beside the fact that she had fucked her jailer and had enjoyed it. *What am I going to do?*

A knock on the door interrupted her dark thoughts. "Amanda?"

She looked up to see a woman she had never seen before in her door entrance. She was tall, nearly six feet, with voluptuous curves. Her piercing blue eyes and raven's wing black hair gave her an exotic look. She could see lean muscle in the woman's thighs and arms. For some reason, she did not look like she was one of Samir's concubines.

"I'm sorry, do I know you?"

The strange woman looked over her shoulder before stepping inside. She came over and sat next to Amanda, her voice dropping to a harsh whisper. "No. But I must speak to you urgently."

"I'd rather not," Amanda said looking at her with suspicion. "Unless you have some Godiva chocolate with you and a bottle of sparkling wine, please go away."

"Sparkling wine?"

"Yes, to drown my sorrows in." It was clear this woman wasn't much for subtleties.

"Unfortunately I do not. Grant Hamilton sent me."

"Grant? You know Grant?"

The woman nodded. "My name is Tatianna Romanovsky Hamilton. I am the one who left you that note. I'm here to get you out of here."

"I…I don't think I can leave just yet." Amanda blurted out, completely startled by her own words.

"I did not know that you were enjoying this spa visit that much," Tatianna replied sarcastically. Amanda felt the heat of an unwelcome blush creeping up her cheeks. She had to admit, she had sounded less than enthusiastic.

She sat back, embarrassed. "Listen, I don't know who you are and I just found out who I am. So just give me a minute to process."

"Well, who did you think you were?" Tatianna replied curiously.

"Someone, else," Amanda snapped, "I've been suffering from retrograde amnesia."

"I see."

"I seriously doubt you do."

Tati looked at her with a penetrating gaze before responding. "You look healthy, so you haven't been beaten or starved. You have your own room with no additional guards, so you have been treated like a guest. Your rosy lips indicate you have been recently kissed, continuously. The love bites on your neck confirms this observation. The embarrassed blush on your cheeks completes the picture." Amanda squirmed at the stab of guilt that accompanied Tatianna's words. The Russian continued to look at her expressionlessly.

"Like I said – I see. However, your fiancée and my husband are waiting not far from here to take this estate, by force if need be. I think it would be better for all of us if we skipped the violence and just snuck out of here instead."

"I...yes you are right." Taking a deep breath Amanda decided getting out of her gilded cage was more important than her mixed emotions.

"Good. Let's go." Before any additional words were said, the door cracked open again and two armed men dressed in black, and wearing masks walked in. They looked dangerous and far from friendly.

"Amanda do you know these men?" Tatianna asked, eyes fixed on their visitors.

"No, I have never seen them before," Amanda replied, moving so she was standing behind Tati. The taller man took a step towards them.

"Ladies, don't make this harder than it needs to be," he said snickering. "Mind you, I don't know how my cock could get any harder." Their masked visitors chuckled. Tatianna swayed her hips, remaining silent.

"High class hookers, like you girls, are hard to find in the desert," the man continued. "James, lock the door."

"What for?" His companion asked, mesmerized by Tati's hip movements.

"I think we have time to enjoy ourselves before getting to business." The attacker in front of Tati looked smug and lowered his weapon. "Isn't that the redhead, the girl the boss was looking for?"

"I think you are right, but he never did say anything about snatching her intact."

The assailant tucked his gun into his belt. "I don't think I will need this, I think my 'tool' will be enough." They both laughed as if he had said something extremely funny. The second man followed suite and tucked his weapon away as well.

"Stay behind me," Tatianna said to Amanda, without seeming the least bit stressed by the situation. Amanda obeyed without hesitation, her eyes desperately scanning the room for anything to use as a weapon. The shorter man started circling the women whistling appreciatively. He could have just gone for the gun he had set aside, but it was clear that for the moment he had forgotten about his mission and was more intent on satisfying his perverted urges.

"Ah, you are feisty little things. This will make it even more enjoyable."

The tall man made a burst towards Tati; she moved smoothly out of the way and drove her fist into his throat, effectively clotheslining him. He went down hard, his body hitting the floor in a sickening thud. This had the second man pausing.

"So, not so helpless after all. Well, let's just see how good you really are."

The man shifted his weight to the balls of his feet, eyes fixed on Tatianna. When the attack came Amanda was totally unprepared, and had to frantically scoot back to get out of the way. With wide eyes she watched the deadly dance that was taking place in front of her. Both opponents where evenly match. The henchman had superior strength, but Tatianna had speed and agility and she put it to use; expertly dodging his fists and kicks.

As the hand-to-hand combat became even more intense Amanda looked frantically around for anything she could use to help. That's when she spotted the gun, still tucked away in the first assailant's pants. As she picked it up, she aimed at the attacker and got a shot off that shattered a vase. The room went silent.

"Hands up. Or the next bullet will be in your head."

"You don't want to be playing with toys you don't know how to use little girl," the man replied threatening, and started moving towards her.

"Listen asshole, I've had a very bad couple of months. I am NOT IN THE MOOD!" she shouted. He stopped dead in his tracks. "Hands up or I WILL shoot you. Who knows, with any luck I will miss and shoot your balls off instead?" Amanda was shaking uncontrollably.

"You don't look too experienced with that gun, little lady."

Tati walked up to Amanda and took the gun away from her. She cocked it and pointed it at the assailant. "Well I can promise you I certainly know how to shoot. On your knees."

CHAPTER 5

The next minutes were some of the longest of Amanda's life. They had quickly tied up their would-be-attackers but now came the challenge of making it out unseen. Unlocking the door, both women tried to act inconspicuous, keeping their veils over their faces and trying to act unassuming. They didn't get very far though before they bumped into Nadia. Accurately assessing her as a threat Tatianna quickly assumed a fighting stance, when Nadia held up her hands. "Peace Amazon, I am not here to stop you." She moved swiftly into an alcove, beckoning them to follow her.

"Nadia, what is going on?" Amanda asked anxiously, reassured despite herself to see a familiar foe.

Nadia turned towards her and whispered. "Keep your voice down. If you draw attention to us, even I cannot stop these invaders from finding you."

"How do you know they are not here to rescue me?"

"No man would send mercenaries to rescue his fiancée in this fashion. Not if he valued her," Nadia replied with an ironic smile. "Furthermore these sons of pigs are disrobing all the girls in search of you. That is when they're not making lewd remarks and threatening rape." As Amanda looked around she finally noticed that women where hurriedly dashing through the quarters.

"But we are not without means to protect ourselves. We have already dealt with a couple of them." Nadia pointed to four women who were trying to drag the lifeless bodies of two men into a corner.

Worry momentarily creased Nadia's brow. "The danger is very real though. For these pigs to have reached our sanctuary they must have disabled or killed the guards." Shaking her head at the thought of it she continued, "We are prepared though."

She ushered them down a small hallway. "Despite being as delicate as flowers, the women in the middle-east were bloomed in the desert, so we are as hardy and as deadly as the Sahara itself. We intend to show these men what a mistake they have made." As Amanda glanced at the bevy of beauties rushing through the hallway she realized that cleverly concealed by veils, in the palm of their hands or skirts were weapon of all sorts, knives, forks, hairpins.

Nadia strode without hesitation to a locked cabinet. "Since it is you they are after, the safest thing for the girls would be if you left, Amanda Cardwell. This is kept for the few times Samir has desired to take any of the harem girls with him overseas," Nadia explained, handing Tati and Amanda jeans and t-shirts. "I apologize if the sizes are not correct."

"It is fine," Amanda replied, pulling her top over her large breasts.

"I will stand as a look out."

After getting dressed, the two women waited, until Nadia came back. "The way is clear. I wish you both luck," Nadia said, embracing Amanda abruptly. "I hope you do not think ill of me."

"I...I don't. Thank you for helping me." Nadia nodded.

"I wish you Godspeed. Now, run swiftly down this corridor, the second door has a fake candle holder, pull it. It is a concealed door. A secret tunnel for the Masters nightly visits. At the intersection of the tunnel, take a right to navigate your way towards the fleet of vehicles. The exit is just a stone's throw away from the garage.

Hurrying through the halls, Tati kept them both at a swift pace. "When I get back to the States, promise me you're going to make sure I start doing my workouts again," Amanda huffed. As they emerged from the tunnel the women were momentarily blinded, their relief at being out quickly dissipating as two masked men materialized like genies to block their entry into the garage hanger.

"This is becoming a very energetic day," Tatianna commented drily.

"Energetic? Eh, I guess you could say that. I was going to go with shitty, crappy, and disastrous," Amanda replied without missing a beat.

Gunfire sounded in the far distance but both women focused on the men about to pounce on them. However, before anything else went down both men were struck from behind.

As they crumbled to the ground, Amanda's breath left her lungs in a long rush. She went very still, every muscle locked, frozen. There he was, her shadow man, *Grant Hamilton*.

How could she have forgotten how handsome he was? Her memories of him crystalized in an intense wave that staggered her.

24

She almost ran to him. But she was assaulted by memories of Samir's lovemaking crashing in on an ocean of guilt. Instead she gazed at him in despair. Shuffling her feet she let her eyes stray and noticed he was standing next to a man who bore a family resemblance. She could only assume this was Alexander Hamilton. As the men stepped up to them, Amanda bit her lip until it was throbbing in tandem with her pulse.

"Hi Amanda," Grant said hesitantly.

"Hi…" she replied eyes staring at her feet. As he reached out and caressed the tendril of her hair that had fallen in front of her face, her heart did a summersault.

"I am sorry it took so long to come and get you." His words were delivered in a soft whisper.

"That's ok. Thank you for coming." Unable to resist his towering presence, with a sob, she walked into his arms.

***

Alexander watched his brother's reunion, pleased the mission looked to be a success. But as he looked around, he was very much aware they were still in enemy territory and not out of the woods yet. Keen to give his brother a few seconds of privacy he walked up to his wife marveling at how she could still take his breath away. "Hi darling, did you miss me?" he asked, before kissing her thoroughly. Smiling she whispered back, "Yes."

Alex turned to his brother, who was still holding his fiancée. "Ok boys and girls we need to get out of here stat."

His wife nodded. "Let's split up. This way they will have to track more than one target, this will undermine their efforts."

"Good idea," Alex replied turning towards his brother. "Grant here are the coordinates for our rendezvous point. The extraction is in 39hrs from now. Stay off any mobile communication devices, as these might have been compromised."

We are exiting the compound in two black jeeps. Give us some cover, Alex radioed the rescue team.

"No one is leaving here without my permission," said a calm voice. Sheikh Samir Ben Alid, Yusef, and two other guards emerged from the secret tunnel.

As Grant's eye settled on his one-time schoolmate the rage he had been containing burst. He took up a sprint and without slowing down he plowed into Samir. They both went down hard, Grant aiming a kick at Samir's face.

As they rolled, kicking and punching, Samir got the upper hand with a well-aimed kick in the stomach. As Grant propelled backwards, grunting, they both eyed each other viciously before getting up and circling around one another. Samir feigned a right punch only to swing around with a roundhouse kick. Grant blocked and delivered a punch straight into Samir's face. He then ducked under his raised fists and delivered three consecutive blows under his ribcage.

Samir's guards joined the fight, but they soon found themselves having to face off against Tatianna and Alexander Hamilton. The fighting started in earnest.

Amanda didn't know what to do. She stood in the eye of the storm, violence erupting all around her. Her heart was thumping, strained beyond endurance. She hadn't had any time to process all the things that had happened. This confrontation with Samir was too soon. As Grant finally got the upper hand and pointed a gun at Samir, she found her voice.

"STOP!" she screamed at the top of her lungs. Everyone stilled.

THE TYCOON'S REPLACEMENT BRIDE - PART 3

Without any hesitation, eyes staring firmly at Samir, she started walking towards him. As Grant tried to hold her back she shook off his hand, and didn't slow down. She could feel a single hot tear run down her cheek.

"*Habibi*, I never meant to make you—"

Smack!

The slap, delivered so precisely, rang like a bell in the hanger. The silence that followed it was deafening.

"We are leaving." Without another word she turned around and walked back to Grant.

Sir we had the assailants pinned down but they are now on the move towards your position. The radioed message echoed.

"Come on Grant. That's our queue, we've gotta go." Grant was breathless with rage. The desire to finish Samir off, was gnawing at him. But as he looked at Amanda's crestfallen face, he knew this was not the time or the place. Reluctantly he lowered his gun.

"Samir, rest assured this isn't over yet. We will settle this soon." His voice laced with menace.

"*Inshallah* (if God wills it)," Samir answered.

"Don't worry, he does," replied Grant.

Gunfire started to increase outside, prompting both couples to jump into the nearest parked jeeps.

"We will see you at the rendezvous point. Don't be late." With those final words, Alex sped away, Grant hot on his tail.

As they drove off the grounds Amanda looked back, and could see Samir, staring at them his hands clenched at his side. Her heart clenched. Unflinching she kept her eyes on him until they were out of view. She sighed deeply and longed for the days when her biggest problem was a two-timing, married cheat.

***

The roar in Grant's head refused to quiet down. He had noticed how well she looked. However, more importantly, he had noticed how her gaze had lingered on that bastard Samir. That simple gesture laid a dagger of ice into his heart.

However, now was not the time to untangle his mixed emotions, they were still in danger. Veering west, away from the estate he watched as his brother veered east. Using years of hard-won discipline, he took deep breaths until all that was left in his mind was the need to get to their escape point intact.

As they sped away, all that could be seen along the road was mile after mile of desolate desert. Flashing by on either side of the road where sparse patches of scorched scrub, prickly pear cactus, and the occasional, sorry-looking *retama* flower. The wind tore through the vast expanse, sweeping sand along the ground. Grant looked in his rear view mirror and saw a black SUV was approaching at breakneck speed. They were being pursued.

"Shit!" The word came out involuntarily.

"What is it?" Amanda queried

"We've got company." Grant's forehead wrinkled in concern.

"These can't be Samir's men," Amanda exclaimed, turning back in her seat to get a better look.

"Most likely not. Do you know what these guys are after and why they are pursuing us?"

"I know they are after me, as to why, I haven't got a clue."

Grant pressed down on the accelerator.

"They are gaining on us!" Amanda shouted, holding on for dear life. The SUV quickly caught up to them. Two menacing thugs, dressed like the other men that had attacked the estate, were inside.

"I can see that," muttered Grant. The SUV drove into the back of the jeep, jarring them both.

Grant knew the longer they stuck to the road the quicker they would be overrun. However, their pursuers SUV wouldn't fare so well across the sandy dunes of the Sahara, at least not as well as the Jeep Wrangler he was driving. "Hang on to your seat. This ride is about to get even bumpier." He shifted gears and tried to pull away from their pursuers.

One of the thugs leaned out of the passenger side window with a handgun that had a silencer attached to it. Looking decidedly smug, he started target practicing on the jeep. The first shot went high, missing the 4x4 by a couple of inches. The mercenary readjusted his grip, aimed and shot towards the jeep again. The sharp shards of the interior mirror shattering missed Grant's face by a centimeter as the bullet went through the windshield. Grant tried again to pull away from the SUV, but their pursuers were sticking close, trying to push their car off the road. Now almost side-by-side, the SUV slammed into the side of the Jeep. As he maneuvered away, Grant struggled to retain control. The two vehicles were fast approaching a bend in the road. Grant did not remove his foot from the accelerator…

"Grant, we are approaching a curve!"

"I know, hold on."

As the SUV and jeep sped down the middle of the road, approaching the pin curve Grant suddenly slammed the jeep into the side of the other car. As the vehicles approached the turn at the last second he pulled the handbrake so the vehicle did a 180° spin. The maneuver nearly tipped the car over. The SUV, unprepared for the move, in its haste to get out of the way swerved into the uneven desert terrain and was violently flipped into the air. Without a glance back to see what happened to their assailants Grant drove the jeep off the road and into the desert at high speed.

Soon the sparse desert landscape turned into soft sand and they were driving amongst the sand dunes. Grant struggled to ensure the vehicle went up the sand dunes, but the 4x4 drifted sideways as if they were on a boat. The sensation was disorientating.

The dunes were fragile and soft, and initially the jeep just veered through them. However half an hour into their drive the car started sputtering.

"What's wrong?" Amanda asked anxiously. The sputtering suddenly ceased and the vehicle started to slow down.

As Grant checked the cars dials, he couldn't believe their bad luck. "We are out of gas. I think one of the bullets shot a hole in our tank."

They were stranded in the middle of the desert.

CHAPTER 6

Amanda watched quietly as Grant unbuckled himself and started rummaging through the jeep.

"What are you looking for?"

"Provisions. This car was parked not far from the garage entrance, it could well have been provisioned for a short trip." As he searched through the car, Grant reemerged with a smile.

"Bingo, two small bottles of water, a blanket and a couple of chocolate bars."

"That doesn't sound like a treasure to me."

"You'll change your mind once you've been out in the desert for a while." He reached inside his pocket and took out a map and a compass. Using the inbuilt GPS in the car he jotted down their location and then proceeded to smash the device.

Turning to Amanda he said, "Let's go."

"Go where? We are in the middle of the desert," she reminded him.

"We can't stay here. Notwithstanding the fact that those goons will likely come back once they have a better equipped vehicle, this water will not last us in midday desert temperatures. We might very well die from dehydration before they ever get to us."

"But go where?"

"To our meeting point. It is only a couple of miles away. Use your veil as a head band to protect against heat stroke. If the heat doesn't kill you in the desert during the day, the cold at night will. This is why we need to go right now, to make enough headway."

"Were you a desert Bedouin in a previous life?" Amanda asked, eyebrow raised.

"Nope, but I did come out top of my class in the Boy Scouts," Grant relied with a reassuring smile.

They started their trek under the sunset, the silence between them was decidedly uncomfortable. As Grant watched Amanda through the corner of his eye, the need to ask her if she had been hurt gnawed at him. His brief glimpse of her curvy body in her harem getup seemed to imply no visible physical damage. But what had happened between her and Samir?

"Did he hurt you?" The words were blurted out without any finesse. The silence that followed was deafening. Amanda closed her eyes, desperately wishing she could take back the events of the last couple of weeks.

"No, not physically he didn't."

"So he didn't rape you?"

"No."

Grant's relief was immediate, but as he gazed intently at Amanda he realized there was something else she was holding back. He remembered the romantic pictures he had seen of her and Samir. Finally, he asked the question that had secretly been plaguing his mind, "Did you sleep with him?"

Amanda did not know what to say. There was no way she could answer this question without hurting Grant. As the sun disappeared at the horizon, she knew the only way was to be truthful. "Until Tatianna Hamilton burst into my room earlier today I didn't know who I was. I didn't know who you were or that I had been kidnapped. I thought I was there of my own free will."

Grant's gut knotted. He could hear the thud of his heart pounding in his ears, like the roar of a wounded animal.

"What are you trying to say?"

"Yes, I slept with him."

Her admission triggered something vicious and dark in him. He turned away from her and walked away. His hands clenched into tight fists, and his heart summersaulting erratically.

Amanda ached as she watched his retreating back. Samir's betrayal still stung like an open wound. Although he had coaxed her consent, the truth of their relationship had her feeling emotionally violated.

She didn't feel clean anymore. She wasn't surprised Grant walked away. She wanted to walk away from herself. Based on the ridged set of his shoulders she knew he was angry. Feeling like an abandoned puppy she wrapped her arms around herself and started walking after him.

By the time night set, the desert was a cold, barren place. Grant had been acting as if she was leper all evening. Keeping conversations to short, curt responses and waking as far ahead as possible.

They were both visibly exhausted. Amanda's mouth was as dry as parchment despite taking small sips of water from her bottle throughout the day.

"Let's camp here for the night." These were the first words to come out of Grant's mouth voluntarily. Looking around warily, all Amanda could see apart from sand, was a large, desert rock. But as exhausted and dehydrated as she was, she didn't care where they stopped as long as they stopped. As she was about to go lie down on the other side of the rock Grant grabbed her hand.

"No. The sun rises in the east. We need to sleep west of the rock to be in the morning shade." With no further conversation he pulled her down next to him, covered them both with the blanket and went to sleep. Amanda was awake for what felt like an eternity. The warmth of Grant's body sent a rush of electricity sparkling across her skin. She didn't understand how she could have forgotten this. The mere scent of him had her squirming. *Stupid girl. You will probably die in this desert. Stop thinking about sex.* Safe in his embrace, she finally fell asleep.

***

The desert lay still under the morning sunrise, the lazy swirling of a distant dust devil the only movement to be seen. Grant was awake. He had been for hours. Taking a deep breath, he turned around and finally looked at the woman he had come to save.

His golden gaze devoured her face, taking in every shadow, noting how dry her lush lips had become. It was clear they needed to get out of this desert, the quicker the better. Determined, they would not die a million miles from home, he turned towards Amanda.

"Wake up. We need to leave, very soon." While Amanda shook the sleep from her eyes, Grant checked his compass. When they had broken down, the car's GPS app had estimated that they had another 25 miles to go before they reached the rendezvous point. At the rate they were moving, factoring in the fact they could not travel at high noon and would likely have to zigzag through mountainous, sand dunes, they had another day's worth of walking ahead of them.

***

20 Miles later

"Is this it? Have we reached the rendezvous point?"

"Yes it is just past this ridge."

Amanda nodded. Her clothes were in taters, her mouth as dry as parchment. If it hadn't been for Grant's encouragement during their trek through the hot, furnace desert she would have given up a long time ago.

If she could have, she would have cried out of relief, but she was too dehydrated to do even that. As they reached the pinnacle of the ridge they could see the rescue helicopter waiting for them. "Come on," Grant shouted grabbing her hand. They started to run towards the helicopter. A tall man, with broad shoulders, sandy brown hair, dark brown eyes flecked with lighter specks, and a carbine machine gun in his hands, stepped out of the side door of the UH-60. "Mr. and Mrs. Hamilton," he shouted.

"Yes, we are the Hamiltons!" Grant shouted back.

"We are your ride home," the pilot yelled. "This area isn't secure we need to get airborne as quickly as possible!"

Grant nodded, and guided Amanda into the waiting chopper. Helping her in, he strapped her into a jumpseat in the back.

"Where are my brother and his wife?"

"They are waiting for you at basecamp. Mr. Hamilton

sustained a flesh wound during the initial escape."

As soon as they were belted in, the pilot pulled back on the control stick, and the chopper shot into the air, banking quickly before heading out towards the ocean.

An armed guard sat at the entrance of the chopper, manning a mounted machine gun. As the chopper blades whined overhead taking them to safety, Amanda wondered if things were ever going to be the same again.

CHAPTER 7

2 weeks later Hamptons, New York

Alexander Hamilton stood next to his brother, reaching for the remote control in his hand. "Jesus Grant, do you really need to keep torturing yourself?"

Grant snatched his arm away, giving his brother a withering stare. "I need to know, Alex. Just how far it went."

"For fuck's sake, she had amnesia! She barely remembered her name the whole time. Combine that with physical stress, emotional displacement, and a bunch of other things that let's just say the CIA taught me more about than I ever wanted to know in my life, and yes, things probably got a bit steamy between them."

Grant ignored his brother, and turned his attention back to the video monitor. He clicked the play button on the remote, and watched as Samir tweaked Amanda's nipple through her silken harem top. She leaned back, her legs spreading in want. The bastard continued to nibble and suck at her neck, before he reached between her legs. She pushed away, kicking at him, before what looked like tears came to her eyes and she stumbled, falling to the floor. The scene continued, but Grant turned away, his emotions in turmoil.

It had been two weeks since Amanda's rescue. Every time he looked at her, he felt like his heart had been ripped from his chest. Shame and anger were waging a war within him. Shame, that he let her be taken. Anger, that there might have been something more than a jailer/kidnapper relationship between her and Samir. He was plagued with thoughts that she actually cared for him. And that shamed him more than else.

What if she wished she were still back with him? The lost look in her eyes every time they were together made him blaze with futile rage. He knew the logic of it, she was innocent, but his bruised heart was aching at the images he was seeing.

He didn't know what to do with his anger. Never mind how much he denied it out loud he WAS angry at her, but he was even angrier at himself and at Samir. Fuck! He was angry at the whole damned world and he didn't know how to stop.

"Why has Samir got it in for you like a bad rash?" Alexander asked. "I can only imagine he is the one who sent you this tape."

"The package was anonymous, but who else? He probably orchestrated the kidnapping because of what happened with Amirah." Grant replied, his eyes cold as icicles.

"His sister? Why'd you dump her, anyway?" Alexander asked, looking bewildered. "You didn't go about it in the most subtle of way. What did she do?"

Grant ran a hand through his hair, breathing shakily as he struggled to control his emotions. "She didn't do anything wrong. It's just that.... well.... she wasn't my type."

"When you dumped her, you shamed the eldest daughter of a Muslim Middle Eastern oil baron. Jesus Grant, that was some stupid shit," Alex said, "You fucked a virgin, the eldest sister of one of your rivals, and let her go. I'm surprised this didn't bite you in the ass years ago." Grant didn't bother responding.

"Did you hurt her?" Alex asked softly.

"No, dammit!" Grant retorted vehemently, spinning to face his brother. Trying to calm down he took a deep breath and responded, "The irony is I never touched her."

"What?" Alex almost choked on his gin and tonic.

"You heard me, I didn't touch her. Amirah and I were dating platonically for a couple of weeks, but we both knew it wasn't going anywhere. One night I found her disheveled and sobbing on the estate grounds. She had been sleeping with some millionaire shit-head who after taking her virginity that very night had dumped her. I promised never to tell. Everyone just assumed since the two of us were dating, I was the culprit in the story. Samir was always a patient, vindictive man," Grant explained, a muscle flicking angrily at his jaw. "Listen Alex, I know I got lucky. And I'm thankful for your help as well as Tati's. But this is out of your hands now. Clearly the sick S.O.B is playing some twisted game."

"Twisted is a mild way of putting it. Does Amanda know you have this tape?"

"No, and I want to keep it that way. Now don't you have a bombshell of a wife to get back to?"

Alexander came over and gave his brother a hug, slapping him on the back. "Hang in there big brother. I am sure between Chase and Jake's efforts you will nail the bastard where it hurts."

Grant returned the hug. "Thanks, Alex. Now, get out of here

before I throw you out."

Alexander let go of his brother, looking him in the eye. "Just promise me you'll talk to me before you think of doing anything else completely stupid, okay?"

"Sure, I will stick to only slightly stupid."

Grant grimaced, and Alexander shook his head and left. As soon as Grant was alone in his library, he hit the play button again. Outside, the moon over the Gulf of Mexico set, and the night birds cried out in the Florida darkness.

***

"Emma, I don't know what to do." Desperate for advice Amanda had locked herself in the study with her favorite gadget, the iPhone. She was having a face-to-face conference with Emma Baker, her best friend.

"I thought you guys had sorted it by now. According to the media you had some kind of daring rescue and your fairytale wedding was back on."

"The media announcement and photo-shoots were just for show. We haven't been intimate since I got back."

"What do you mean you haven't been intimate? Not even a peck on the cheek?"

"No."

"Hand holding?"

"No."

"Does he know about you and Samir?"

"I told him we slept together."

"Damn, you are in deep shit."

"Yep that's me. Up shit creek without a paddle," Amanda

replied as she curled up on the sofa in the study. Despite her spunky words she felt bereft and alone. Everything was so different now between her and Grant.

"What were you thinking? A man will forgive anything, but after frantically looking for you all over the world, finding out you are playing lovers with your kidnapper is probably not one of them."

"Ems you know it wasn't like that. It has taken me the last couple of weeks to stop wanting to wring Samir's neck," Amanda replied with a sigh. What she didn't want to admit, even to her best friend was how she still felt dirty and now so unworthy of Grant's love. She had a hard enough time admitting it to herself.

"So we can conclude you are not in love with tall, dark, and dangerous then?"

"I can't believe you even bothered stating the *blatantly obvious*. What happened with Samir was way worse than Scott, the two-timing bastard. At least with Scott, it was my decision, *me*, Amanda, not some amnesic girl scammed into a sexual romp. I might have been confused right after I found out, but I'm over it."

"Calm down, I was just asking, jeez."

"Ems, I just want Grant back, and I don't know what to do so he wants to be with me again," Amanda replied in a tear-smothered voice.

"Calm down. You are just going to have to do anything and everything."

"What do you mean?"

"Amanda, do you know the lengths Grant went to, to get you guys together? I am not just talking about rushing across the world and saving you from some sex fiend. That in itself is worth a medal, but the length he went through before you even met. I mean, he took one look at you in my summer pictures and that was it. He had to meet you. Once I showed him our crazy videos he was even more adamant. If I hadn't thought you guys would be a match made in heaven I wouldn't have gone along with his scheme to lure you to his mansion." Emma's word felt like a soothing balm over Amanda's raw nerves.

"The guy fell madly in love with you, even before meeting you. The question is this, do you love him as madly? If you do, then you need to do anything and everything to make him forget your unwanted liaison with Samir. Remind him he loves you."

"How the heck do I do that?"

"Well you could start by talking to him, instead of talking to me. Swiftly followed by a rumble in the haystack and that should get you guys back on the right track."

"Thanks Ems, I didn't know you turned into an agony aunt while I was gone?"

"You can thank me at your wedding."

CHAPTER 8

S purred by her conversation with Emma, Amanda decided to take the bull by the horns and seek out Grant. After they returned to the estate he moved into one of the en-suite rooms located on the other side of his mansion. She had never set foot there, but tonight she would seek him out in his private refuge.

"Grant?" she whispered tentatively as she tiptoed into the suite. She made a full stop at the threshold and stared open mouthed. The room was enormous. It had a separate dining area with a side entrance to the main sleeping area. There was a mahogany, four-poster bed centered in the room and the entire wall opposite the bed was covered in a gigantic mirror.

"Grant? Are you here?" With apprehension, she walked further into his bedroom.

"What are you doing here?" At the sound of Grant's less than pleased tone Amanda whipped around and caught her breath. He stood at the entrance of the room, with only a towel around his waist, his torso still slightly damp from his shower. He looked breathtakingly handsome.

"I was just…eh. I wanted to have a chat, but since you are busy I will come back some other time."

Grant shook his head and walked over to the walk-in wardrobe. "This is as good a time as any." Completely ignoring her, he reached for a towel and started drying his hair.

"I just wanted to know if you were up for dinner tonight. Just the two of us down by the lake."

Grant tilted his head, curious. "Oh? Why?"

Amanda pondered her answer for a moment, and chose the least controversial response. "Well, I know these past weeks have been strained," she replied. "And I'm sorry for being so withdrawn. You've been a total gentleman this whole time, and I thought we could get a fresh start."

Grant stared at her silently before responding. "Amanda, I would be more than happy to start again, that said you've got to get yourself checked out first."

"Checked out?" Amanda stated, puzzled.

Grant nodded and looked away. "We should have done it as soon as you got back, but I delayed because I knew you needed some time to reacclimatize to America. But a doctor really should check you out after what you've been through. Who knows if there is any long term danger from that knock to your head, or the drugs you were injected with?" The words *"and your lovemaking to Samir"* hung silently between them.

Unable to stand the tension that was between them, Amanda blurted out, "Why don't you just get it out? I'm tired of this little game we are playing."

"Get what out?" Grant replied, his golden brown eyes staring

44

intensely into hers.

"Whatever it is that you've been dying to say."

"Really?" Grant's reply was delivered as soft as a dangerous whisper, promising her, wherever she was taking this conversation she really didn't want to go there.

A wave of despair swept through her. She wished she could break down the walls that were keeping them apart. That he would kiss her, slip inside her, and forget the events that had separated them.

Realizing that she would have to push the subject or maybe forever lose him, Amanda took her courage in hand and pressed on. "You haven't touched me since we got back."

Her words hung between them like a silent condemnation. Grant put aside his second towel and walked towards her. He didn't stop until she was near enough to feel the heat of him. Amanda gulped.

"Touched you? You want me to touch you?" His gaze trailed along her alabaster neck, down to her creamy heaving bosom.

"Who am I to refuse? If the lady wants to be touched, touched you shall be." With no additional warning, he swung her around, pressing her back firmly against the hard length of him. There was no mistaking his desire for her. His member could have been made out of marble.

"Grant, what are you doing?" Amanda whispered, breathlessly.

"Touching you. Isn't that what you requested?" His warm breath was sending tendrils of hot desire down her spine.

"Do you want me to touch you here?" his fingers grazed her puckered nipple. "Or here?" He ground his cock against her backside. "Is that rough enough or would you like it rougher, like your Arabian lover."

At his vicious words Amanda tore herself free and turned around to face him. "He wasn't my lover by choice and you know it."

"It didn't stop you from enjoying it *darling*." And there it was, her secret shame. The wall that was between them finally crystalized.

She could not deny the pleasure that Samir had given her, and for that she was still cursing his name.

"Never mind, this conversation is pointless. I will leave you to it," Amanda retorted and started walking towards the exit. She barely took a step, before she was roughly pulled into Grant's arms again, his lips crushing hers in a bruising kiss. Although she should have been outraged, a small part of her was just relieved to feel him against her. She'd been so afraid he'd never want to touch her again.

"When he kissed your lips did he make you feel like this?" Grant muttered, as he continued his punishing exploration.

"Grant don't. Please stop. Not like this, not in anger. Please." Even as the words left her lips, her body was betraying her, her nipples straining for his attention. He lifted up her skirt and without hesitation inserted his chunky finger in her wet sheet. Amanda's legs buckled.

"When he fucked you did you juice as much as you are juicing for me?" Grant's words were laced with torment.

"Please stop," Amanda moaned.

"Did you tell HIM to stop, or were you enjoying yourself too much?" *How did you not know you were mine?*

"I…I can't change anything that happened. And I can't deny that he didn't force himself on me. But that was before – before I knew," she whimpered.

THE TYCOON'S REPLACEMENT BRIDE - PART 3

Her words nearly shattered him. He knew what it was like to fill her, to stretch her. He knew what it was like to have her ride him, slick with hot heat, and he resented that any other man before or since him had ever made a claim on her. It was irrational, unfair but her pleading voice could not assuage his anger… his shame.

"I can't deny I wanted you from the very first moment I saw you," he whispered in her ear, while his digit continued to slowly fuck her.

"If you want to be with me, this is all I have left to offer you." He inserted a second digit into her tight tunnel and used his left hand to stroke her nipple. "*Need, hunger, possession.*" Amanda found herself juicing copiously, the muscles in her stomach starting to clench. She knew this was punishment. He was deliberately using sex against her, but her body remembered how a mere touch from him could solicit intense pleasure. As he claimed her mouth with his, she didn't have the willpower to resist; instead her fingers fisted in his hair, holding him to her. She closed her eyes and savored the feel of his tongue and the heat of his mouth as he suckled her lower lip. He wasn't gentle, his teeth scrapping against hers, but her body reacted with an urgency that had her nearly sobbing.

"Did he make you feel like this? Did you get wet for him, dammit?" his words were growled like an animal in pain. Abruptly he stepped away from her. Panting they stared at each other. His next sentence was uttered without a shred of emotion.

"Your total submission is what I *crave*. Give it to me, or get the hell out of my bedroom." His glittering eyes met hers, cold, possessive, and utterly without mercy. Her pulse began a frantic rhythm.

Amanda knew she had to make a decision. It was now or never. If she denied him they might never be able to bridge what had happened. When she closed her eyes it wasn't Samir's brown eyes she glimpsed inside her mind. It was hazel eyes, blazing with determination, Grant's eyes. She stilled. Suddenly she knew without a shadow of a doubt she would do anything to be with him. She looked at Grant and nodded as she touched her tongue to her tender lips. That was all the permission Grant needed.

Grabbing a hold of her like a drowning man to a lifeboat, he claimed her lips again, forcefully starting an erotic dance with their tongues as the main players. Amanda's body went up in flames. As he took command, one fist in her thick auburn hair, he forced her head back, his tongue dueling with hers. He plundered her mouth, and she couldn't think a coherent thought. All she knew was that she wanted more.

When he pulled away from her, she had trouble catching her breath. How she had missed this. Through just one kiss he was more addictive than any other man she had ever met or been with.

Panting Grant stared at her, determination written all over his face. "Take off your clothes and get on the bed on all fours." His voice brokered no argument. Committed she walked slowly to the bed. As she shed her clothes, she could feel the heat of his gaze burning her. Wearing only her cotton underwear, she climbed on to the bed and went on all fours.

She watched him in the mirror as he removed the towel around his hips and dropped it on the floor. He was magnificent. His cock jutting out like a sword, ready to conquer. The sight of him had her salivating.

He walked towards a chest of drawers and emerged with a riding crop. She stared wide-eyed. What did he intend to do with that? Her racing heart doubled in pace. She was determined not to run or cry, whatever may happen, so she stayed put.

He paced up to her, the riding crop in one hand. As her eyes met his, she knew what was to come might require more than total submission. His desire was set to devour her, mind, body, and soul. She knew she welcomed it. She *needed* it.

As he got closer, Amanda shut her eyes bracing herself for what was to come. She knew he felt betrayed, but she had never thought this would be the price she had to pay.

As irrational as it was, it was her shame that kept her in place on all fours. She had a twisted desire to do penance. She needed to be cleansed in the flames of his passion, to make it right, for both of them.

Since it was clear total submission was the only penance he would accept. She was more than willing to pay, if only so that he would love her again, just a little, as he had before.

.

CHAPTER 9

Grant had never wanted a woman more than he wanted Amanda in that moment. As she lay on all fours, her bottom his to command and possess, he knew the punishment he had in store for her would inevitably torment them both and provide ultimate satisfaction.

Grant wished things could have been different. When he had first devised the plan to make her his bride, he had good intentions. He had intended to show her his gentle side. He would cage the beast that lived inside him. Cage it until they knew each other more intimately. Teach her the darker, more erotic play in increments. Make her slowly understand his need for sexual control.

For a while, he had thought it would work. Then Samir had taken her. Taken what was his. His need for her total submission now blazed like an inferno. The only way to quench the fire was to let it burn.

Although his conscience was screaming to him to stop the path he was on, she was a weakness he was not man enough to walk away from. He was going to show her who she belonged with. Make her yearn and ache. Make her crave his touch and ruin her for everyone else *forever*. She was his and he intended to make sure she knew it. If he could, he would have claimed her very soul. Instead, he intended to possess her in a way Samir never had. *Completely.*

Grant crawled onto the bed, sitting down on his knees between Amanda's legs. He didn't touch her, just trailed the leather tip of the riding crop over the expanse of her creamy thighs.

Amanda's heart began beating frantically. Her eyes widened as he opened up the lips of her labia, eased through the folds, scooping up her creamy wetness and spreading it delicately around her entrance. The pleasure was instantaneous and intense. She closed her eyes and moaned.

"Look at me, look at what I am doing to you," he whispered tersely in her ear. She opened her eyes and looked. The image was beyond erotic. She looked wanton. She should have been ashamed but she wasn't. She wanted this man with every fiber of her being.

He grabbed a hold of her panties and pulled them to the side. The thought of what he was looking at, had her blushing. Eyes riveted to the mirror she watched him devour her womanhood with his gaze. Amanda swallowed hard.

Gazing at her hotly, Grant unhooked her bra, and her big creamy breasts bounced free. "My cock has hungered for only you over the last couple of months. It won't hunger for anyone else anymore." His hand still holding her briefs pulled to the side, he took his member in his other hand and positioned it at her entrance. "As only your body will do, your body is mine." That was all the preparation she had. Not bothering to pull her panties off, he moved, ramming her hard, balls deep. Amanda gasped at the delicious intrusion, her tight channel stretching achingly to accommodate all of him. Her eyes glazed over with feverish need.

"From now on you are mine baby doll. Mine to fuck whenever and however I want," Grant whispered in her ear. He moved back and rammed his cock into her again, hard. Her stomach muscles clenched. "I will spread your legs every morning and deposit my seed deep inside you." She sobbed as he drove his stiff member so deep into her she thought he would fuse them together. Her desire for his possession spurred her to spread her legs even wider.

"There isn't an inch of your body I won't know intimately. My needs are yours to satisfy, as yours are mine. And satisfy them I will." His strong hands held her hips still so she could only submit to receiving his deep invasion. The coil in her stomach tightened.

He pumped his shaft hard into her tunnel. Her juices flowed liberally, soaking the underwear she was still wearing. She wondered how she could ever have thought anyone else could ever compare. It was heavenly. His complete possession of her, made her want to weep with joy, despite the anger that spurred it.

He rode her. Hard. Relentlessly.

"What's my name?" he asked pumping his cock as deep as he could.

"Grant," she groaned.

"And who do you want?" He was now fucking her so thoroughly; his head was pounding her womb. She did not stop juicing.

"Grant, Grant, Grant." She chanted, in a pleading voice that threatened to shatter what was left of his self-control. He pumped into her hard, one last time and simultaneously pinched her clit. Her stomach muscles tightened, and she lost control. Her orgasm swept through her like a tidal wave. As her muscles clenched around his cock Grant almost came. He pulled his jutting tool out of her before the sensations overcame him.

"I am not done with you yet," he muttered. Before she could register what was happening, he grabbed her panties and tore them off her. As he buried his face in her briefs, sniffing the aroma of her come, he muttered gutturally, "You won't be needing this for the rest of the evening baby doll." Amanda's face flushed red and she buried her face quickly in the mattress, too embarrassed to watch.

"It's your sweetness that makes me want to possess you," he whispered as he caressed the back of her head. "Now, spread your legs for me." Amanda gulped, but with her eyes closed did as she was told.

Practiced fingers started swirling around her nub, teasing it with an expert rhythm. It wasn't in the speed. It was in the slightest shift, the way he knew how to arouse her. She groaned. Then the fingers were just gone and a swift, short sting on her clit startled her.

"You didn't think this whip was just for show did you?"

Amanda opened her eyes and looked at the mirror wall. Her panties were now in shreds on the floor and Grant was using the crop, with expert flicks to tap on her pussy. It wasn't hard, not enough to cause her intense pain, but still bites, little bites of pounding against her nub in a completely different way. The pain/pleasure of it was exquisite.

Grant alternated between the crop and his fingers for what felt like forever, until the juices of her wet pussy had stained the bed. Then he stopped.

"Turn around," he commanded. As she lay displayed in front of him, his gaze raked over her naked body and Amanda knew he liked what he saw. Her stomach tightened. He went down between her legs. His finger trailed over her swollen nub and lips, she moaned, desire flowing like molten lava.

"Yes, I think you are almost tender enough. Your lips down here are so beautifully puffy, baby doll." Suddenly he bent over, lifted her legs over her head and licked her swollen mound. She almost flew off the bed. Immobilizing her with one hand he continued to eat her copious juices, as she writhed on the bed. Unable to restrain herself Amanda mewled like a cat and came apart. She convulsed repeatedly as Grant swallowed her delicious creaminess. Spent, she lay limbless on the bed.

Grant's pulse was thudding in his ears, his control on a shoestring. He grabbed a hold of his erection and started massaging it against Amanda's entrance. Exhausted from overstimulation she moaned softly at the intrusion. She hissed in surprise at the girth of his tip as it founds its way between her puffy folds, reaching her achy crevice.

"Your tender pussy feels so good," he muttered. He lubricated his shaft by dipping it in and out of her hot cleft, trembling in his effort to restrain his desire. Her legs over her head, was giving him a heart stopping view of her rear passage. "Your backside is perfection," he grunted. He kneaded her peachy rear – then proceeded to brush a finger between her cheeks. Amanda groaned in protest, still in the grips of her aftermath.

"Shhh," he whispered soothingly, his voice a velvet murmur. His finger didn't stop for an instant caressing her secret entrance.

"Have you ever had a man take you back here baby doll?"

"No," she answered, stains of scarlet appearing on her cheeks.

"Good," he replied, swirling his finger around her knob, then along her pussy lips all the way to her rear passage again. The thought of fucking her there, taking her so completely, made his cock impossibly harder. "It would please me enormously to possess you there. I want to be your first and your last."

Amanda hissed at his admission, at his naked need. Her heart turned over.

"You do want to please me, don't you?"

"Yes." Her whispered confession was laced with longing.

"Good girl."

He proceeded to dip into her sweet cleft, once, twice, the third time he pushed his hard erection gently into her puckered opening. She stilled. Slowly, he rubbed the tip of his shaft against her rear entrance. He returned his hand to her ass cheeks, spreading them widely. Then he pushed his shaft in, one delicious inch at a time. Amanda moaned at the intrusion.

Unrelenting, he pushed harder until finally with a satisfying plop, her anal muscles swallowed the head of his cock and gripped it like a vice.

He trembled as they both remained still, his member throbbing inside her. Her back passage was deliciously hot. The position he had her in meant she was wide open to him, unable to deny him this rare treat, even if she now wanted to. His pelvis rubbed against her engorged clit as he slid further in, headless of the tremor that touched her rosy lips.

Unwilling to deny her desperate desire for his possession, Amanda gritted her teeth against the pain and pushed upwards in an effort to take him even deeper. As the entire length of his hard cock finally pushed through her sphincter and settled firmly in her rear, she revelled in the knowledge she had finally done it, given him every part of her.

As he started administering delicious punishment with his tool, she was soon moaning, incoherently, tearfully, "I am sorry." *Please want me.*

He pulled out of her almost completely, and thrust back in mercilessly. He was opening her up in ways she had never imagined. Her sobs grew in strength. Her pleas an inarticulate prayer, "I will be good." *Please love me.*

His rhythmic pumping only increased in intensity. The pain of his intrusion was delicious; it flowed over her like a healing balm, mingling devilishly with her desire for his full and complete possession. His cock was pumping in and out of her rear balls deep. With each slow, rhythmic motion, she felt cleansed, her body welcoming his ownership. She gave a groan of pain, satisfaction, and pleasure, her anal and stomach muscles tightening in tandem.

Watching her tear up, a secret, dark part of Grant became even more aroused at the dark play she was willing to endure for his pleasure. He could not deny the sweet ecstasy of her submission...he could not...deny his love for her.

He leaned over, his cock deep in her ass and kissed his replacement, mail-order bride passionately. Gutturally he whispered, "You are a *good* girl. You are *my* girl." As he pumped her rear passage, his tongue savored her. Each movement was slow, deliberate, and precise, all with the intention of possessing every inch of her. All with the intention of saying, "I love you. I need you." The harder and deeper he pumped, the longer and sweeter he kissed her.

"I tried to save you," he muttered. "Save you from this beast that lives inside me. The one that wants to devour you. You should have left when you could." He was fucking her ass like a madman. "Now it's too late," he groaned. His cock pounded in and out of her relentlessly, bringing them both to a fever pitch. Then he slipped his hand between her legs and slightly pinched her swollen nub. Amanda's orgasm ripped through her like a tornado, her anal passage spasming around his cock.

Unable to restrain himself any longer, Grant screamed long and hard as he unleashed his seed deep inside her. His orgasm rocked him from head to toe. Exhausted he collapsed on top of her, his cock still twitching, squirting the last load of sperm into her tight passage. Panting, Grant basked in the glow of the greatest sexual experience of his life. He pulled up the blanket and gathered her in his arms.

"I love you Amanda. You are the very air that I breathe and I will never let you go."

More fulfilled than she had ever been in her life, Amanda clung to him, smiling blissfully as she fell asleep.

.

EPILOGUE

Grant Hamilton was at his wedding reception. More accurately, he was in his home office. As he looked at the desktop picture of his beautiful wife, he marveled at the fact, they were now bound together forever. Ever since that night, when Amanda had shown him how far she was willing to go for their love, how completely she was prepared to surrender to him...he had found peace. There was an unspoken agreement between them, never to speak of what had happened. They had both gotten what they needed that evening, the means to heal the rift that had been created between them. He couldn't have been luckier if he tried.

He had a woman that loved him and who relished his darker pleasures. It helped that Amanda enjoyed being his sex slave between the sheets. Though, she still blushed and hid her head in the pillows whenever he tried to pleasure her orally. Little did she understand that her creaminess was like the sweetest nectar to him. Goddess and vixen all rolled into one, now all his. Smiling to himself he turned his attention back to his visitor.

"Is it done?" he asked Jake Hamilton, eager to hear his cousin's report.

"Yes. The fake holdings we set up were a perfect trap. The Ben Alid fortune is about to take a very steep nosedive. I would be surprised if their wealth isn't all but wiped out in the next 6 months."

Grant smiled with satisfaction and shook his cousin's hand. "Thanks cuz." Revenge had been long in coming, but poverty was about to teach a very valuable lesson to Sheikh Samir Ben Alid.

"What about the other matter we discussed. Are you up for it? I know it is not quite your cup of tea."

Jake Hamilton owned a prestigious law firm in Boston. He was known as "The Shark" in legal circles. He was overqualified for grunt work, but he was also the only person Grant could count on to investigate the latest goings on at Hamilton Industries.

Asking him to go undercover at the Hamilton Industries' subsidiary had been Chase's idea. He remembered that Jake had told him how frustrated and bored he was with the types of clients they were receiving.

"Pretending to be a boring junior clerk while trying to uncover the mole at Hamilton Industries that has been selling our tech secrets to the Saudis? Not a problem," Jake replied with a smile. "I could use a break from running my own company."

"I knew I could count on you."

Laughing the cousins hugged and walk out of the meeting room.

AUTHOR NOTE

Thank you so much for reading my book. I love writing and I hope you liked reading this story as much as I liked writing it.

As you probably know, many people look at the reviews on Amazon before they decide to purchase a book. If you liked the book, **could you please take a minute** to leave a review on your local Amazon website with your feedback?

60 seconds is all I'm asking for, and it would mean the world to me.

Thank you so much,

Montana Night

HIS DESIRE FOR HER BLAZED LIKE AN INFERNO

London born Rebecca Martin has spent the last four frustrating years working in the US at CorpSec a private security company catering for the rich and famous. Today, she just got her big break. An opportunity to be wealthy owner Chase Hamilton's personal assistant.

The man is lethal, has a smile to die for and the body and face of a very wicked angel. The attraction is instant, visceral. But she knows he's just too rich, too handsome, too everything to notice the way his plump mahogany replacement secretary has the hots for him. But a case of immigration issues with as Russian mail-order bride is just about to throw her in the path of her tantalizing billionaire boss.

www.amazon.com

HIS PASSIONS WOULD NOT BE DENIED

Billionaire Alexander Hamilton has hidden behind the persona of a dull, fop to deceive the world for so long he rarely shows his true self in public. But Tatiyanna Romanovsky might just be the girl to break down those walls. Ever since they locked heads, his legendary patience has been nowhere to be seen.

When Tati is almost assassinated on US soil Alexander's protective, dominant, possessive male instincts flare to life, leaving him with an intense need to protect and claim this Russian mail-order bride.

www.amazon.com